camp  CONFIDENTIAL

Topsy-Turvy

GROSSET & DUNLAP
Published by the Penguin Group
Penguin Group (USA) Inc., 375 Hudson Street,
New York, New York 10014, USA
Penguin Group (Canada), 90 Eglinton Avenue East, Suite 700, Toronto,
Ontario M4P 2Y3, Canada (a division of Pearson Penguin Canada Inc.)
Penguin Books Ltd., 80 Strand, London WC2R 0RL, England
Penguin Group Ireland, 25 St. Stephen's Green, Dublin 2, Ireland
(a division of Penguin Books Ltd.)
Penguin Group (Australia), 250 Camberwell Road, Camberwell, Victoria
3124, Australia (a division of Pearson Australia Group Pty. Ltd.)
Penguin Books India Pvt. Ltd., 11 Community Centre,
Panchsheel Park, New Delhi—110 017, India
Penguin Group (NZ), 67 Apollo Drive, Rosedale, North Shore 0632,
New Zealand (a division of Pearson New Zealand Ltd.)
Penguin Books (South Africa) (Pty.) Ltd., 24 Sturdee Avenue,
Rosebank, Johannesburg 2196, South Africa

Penguin Books Ltd., Registered Offices:
80 Strand, London WC2R 0RL, England

Cover design by Ching N. Chan
Front cover images © David Woolley/Photodisc/Getty Images, Inc.
and © iStockphoto.com/PeskyMonkey.

Library of Congress Cataloging-in-Publication Data is available.

ISBN 978-0-448-45372-9   10 9 8 7 6 5 4 3 2 1

camp CONFIDENTIAL

Topsy-Turvy

by Melissa J. Morgan

Grosset & Dunlap
An Imprint of Penguin Group (USA) Inc.

chapter
ONE

"Wow," Tricia said with a sigh, leaning back in her chair as she chewed. "You know what I love about bacon, chicas?" She lifted a crackling new strip to her mouth and bit off the end with a loud crunch. "*Everything.*"

Jenna glanced up from her own breakfast, casting a little secret smile over at Natalie. Sometimes it was a little weird having Tricia, the actual First Daughter, as in the *president's* daughter, right there in their tent at camp. But more often, it was just laugh-out-loud funny. Tricia's wacky behavior had been a little hard to take at first, but she was definitely growing on all the girls in the bunk.

"Bacon is pretty awesome," Jenna agreed, finishing up her last piece. "Even the sound it makes cooking sounds like applause. *Sssssssss.*"

Everyone chuckled except Avery, who was supposed to be at home helping her stepmother with her new baby. "You didn't come up with that. You stole that from that comedian, what'shisname—on Comedy Central." Avery claimed her stepmother sent her back to camp halfway through the summer on the grounds that she was being too helpful. But Jenna could only wonder if the real reason behind Avery's return was that she missed having people around to snark at.

Jenna shrugged. "Actually, I stole it from David," she said innocently, gesturing across the mess hall at her good-friend-once-boyfriend, who was sitting with his bunk. "But I wouldn't put it past him to steal a joke. He has no scruples when it comes to comedy."

David caught her eye right at that moment, and gave her a suspicious look—wondering, no doubt, why she was pointing him out to her entire bunk. Jenna just smiled and waved. In response, David shot her an exaggerated glare, then held out his hands with the palms facing up, bouncing them back and forth like he was playing with a Slinky. Then he leaned down to the floor, gesturing like he was pushing something in her direction.

"What's that?" Sarah asked, furrowing her brows.

Jenna sighed. "It's David's way of letting me know I'm in for it. He calls it the Death Slinky. It's coming to kill me or something."

Everyone looked kind of puzzled, but Sarah laughed. "Yeah, that sounds like him," she agreed, happily turning back to her eggs. A waaaayyyy long time ago, before Jenna and David had ever gotten together, Sarah had gone out with him. But that was all ancient history now. Jenna and David had been "just friends" for years.

Jenna turned back to her plate, but she was distracted by Nat, who was giving her a suspicious glance over her orange juice. "What?" Jenna asked.

Nat gestured to David. "You guys have been spending a lot of time together lately."

Jenna swallowed. "Well, David and I have been spending a lot of time trying to figure out the *thing*," she said, clearing her throat in case Nat didn't hear her emphasis. "You know. The . . ."

". . . Strategy for Color War?" Sloan asked brightly, winking in Jenna's direction.

"Exactly," Jenna agreed with a relieved smile. "You know, we want to make sure our team totally kicks butt." She bit her lip, glancing nervously at Jasmine, their counselor. "I mean, wins big. You know. Totally nonviolently."

Jasmine just laughed, shaking her head. Jenna felt a rush of relief. Actually, what she and David had spent so much time talking about had nothing to do with kicking butt at Color War, or anything camp-sanctioned. They had been talking about what Jenna could possibly pull off as her next prank. For all the years Jenna and her friends had been coming to camp together, Jenna had always come up with amazing, elaborate, sometimes punishment-earning pranks. There was the sugar in the saltshakers prank, the fire-engine red hair prank . . . and so many more, really, that Jenna was almost intimidated by her own success. How could she pull off a prank this summer that would really stand out among all of her greatest hits? It was almost impossible to think of something. What Jenna and David had been talking about most recently—after campfire the night before—was that

Jenna probably needed some kind of *outside* assistance to really up the ante. Like if they could get a cool, laid-back counselor in on their scheme. *If* was right. Her chances of getting help from anyone in a position of power were pretty unlikely.

"Hey, check out Dr. Steve," Brynn said, shaking Jenna out of her prank-related trance. "What do you think he's up to?"

Jenna followed Brynn's gaze over to the head of Camp Walla Walla, who was striding up to the podium at the head of the mess hall. When she spotted him, Jenna had to rub her eyes. Was he really—no, he couldn't be.

"Is he wearing *pajamas?*" Priya gasped, covering her mouth to stifle a giggle.

"Oh my gosh," whispered Avery. "This is just like a nightmare I had last week."

"Do you think he realizes it?" hissed Tricia. "This one time, I almost wore my whitening strips to a photo op on the White House lawn. It was only when my mom's secretary pointed it out that I realized I still had them on my teeth!"

"Thank goodness you have assistants," Avery muttered under her breath, not entirely kindly.

"Yeah, thank goodness," Tricia agreed cheerfully, taking another bite of bacon with a sigh. "Ohhhh, last piece."

Jenna grinned as Dr. Steve tapped the mike two times. "Is this thing on?" he asked with a goofy grin, as the campers quickly quieted down. They were all dying to hear his explanation for wearing pj's to breakfast.

"Campers," he continued, "I know you're all eager to get to your morning activities, so I'll keep this brief. Do you notice anything different about me today?"

Laughter spread around the room, reaching near-deafening levels within seconds. "You're wearing your pj's!" squealed one of the youngest campers, a little blond girl with French braids.

"That's right, April!" Dr. Steve said cheerfully. "And what's strange about that?"

April started giggling. In fact, she was giggling so hard, Jenna wasn't sure she'd be able to get the words out. "You're not in bed, silly! You're at breakfast."

Dr. Steve smiled. "That's right," he agreed. "You might even say I'm wearing the . . . *opposite* of what I should be wearing."

Jenna and her friends glanced at one another. "Where's he going with this?" said Priya under her breath.

"And I'm wearing my pj's," Dr. Steve went on, "to announce that tomorrow will be the first official Opposite Day in Camp Walla Walla's history!"

"Opposite Day?" Jenna repeated. She'd been coming to camp—first Lakeview and now Walla Walla—for longer than she could remember, and neither camp had ever done anything like this before.

"Opposite Day will be a new Camp Walla Walla tradition," Dr. Steve explained. "On Opposite Day, everything will be upside down and the opposite of normal! We'll wear our pajamas all day long. We'll have dinner for breakfast. We'll have campfire first thing in the morning. And most exciting . . ."

He paused. The room quieted down instantly, everyone holding their breath to see what the most exciting element would be.

". . . For the first and only time, *campers* will be in charge, and the camp staff and counselors will have to do what you tell us!" The mess hall erupted into cheers, but Jenna heard Dr. Steve lean into the microphone and add, "Within reason, of course."

"Oh, wow," Jenna breathed, instinctively looking over at David, who was staring at her with the same goggle-eyed expression she was sure she wore. "This is perfect!" she mouthed at him.

"Prank to End All Pranks!" David mouthed back.

"There's just one catch," Dr. Steve continued. "There are many more of you than there are of us, as you know."

"Tell me about it," whispered Jasmine, looking less than thrilled about this new development.

"And we need to keep *some* semblance of order around here," Dr. Steve added. "Which means we need some way to choose *one* bunk to be in charge! Which means . . . campwide talent show tonight!"

Jenna pulled her eyes away from David and looked around at her bunkmates. This was her big chance . . . if their bunk was in charge of the rest of the camp tomorrow, she could be responsible for pulling off the biggest prank in history!

Jenna put on her best We've-Got-This expression, but to her surprise, her bunkmates looked less than enthused. Avery looked flat-out bored, but then she often looked that way. Nat looked skeptical. And

Tricia was still having some serious one-on-one time with her bacon.

"We can totally do this," Jenna put in, trying to work up a response from her friends.

"I dunno," Avery said with a shrug. "It's kind of . . . kid stuff, isn't it?"

Nat wrinkled her nose. "Kind of," she agreed. "I mean, pancakes for dinner, whatever, you know?"

"And what do we get to do if we win?" Sloan added. "We could boss the other bunks around, I guess—but so what?"

Jenna felt her eyes bugging out of her head. "*Guys,*" she insisted. "It would be *awesome*. Trust me."

Brynn glanced over at Jenna, and she could tell that Brynn sensed something was up. "Maybe we can talk about it on the way to the lake," Brynn suggested, quickly looking over at Jasmine and Jamie, their counselor and CIT. Jenna nodded, relieved. At least Brynn got it: Jenna had ideas here, *big* ideas, too big to be discussed in the presence of counselors.

"You'll have a couple hours this afternoon to prepare an act," Dr. Steve went on. "Tonight, you'll all draw straws to determine the order of the performances, and the best act will win the chance to rule the camp tomorrow!"

Dr. Steve may have given a few more details, but Jenna was no longer paying attention. She leaped out of her seat and quickly gathered her things, shooting a meaningful look at Brynn, and anyone else who would meet her eye. Within a few minutes, she was outside the mess hall, walking toward the lake. Brynn and the rest of the bunk quickly caught up.

"Okay," Jenna whispered, looking behind her to make sure the counselors were out of earshot. "First things first. We *have* to win tonight. If we win the chance to rule the camp tomorrow, that will give me a chance to pull off an *amazing* prank! Like, legendary!"

Avery sighed. "Jenna, don't you think you're a little old for pranks?"

Jenna turned to her, shocked, but Sarah jumped in before things could get ugly. "Um—pranks are fun for all ages!" she insisted, looking from Avery to Jenna. Sarah had spent a summer at camp with Avery before Jenna and her friends from Camp Lakeview had started coming there, so she had gotten pretty skilled at smoothing over Avery's snarkiness.

"Look at that old Ashton Kutcher show, *Punk'd*. People loved watching that—and not just kids."

"Omigod, you are so *right!*" cried Tricia suddenly, her voice carrying through the woods. "I *love* pranks! Sometimes I like to play little tricks on my secret service guys. Like, I'll try to hide from them and stuff, and see how long I can go before they find me." She paused. "They don't like that too much."

Avery sighed. "I *guess* we can still pull pranks," she muttered, shrugging her shoulders. "But, anyway, even if we *want* to win this thing, it's not guaranteed. We still need a great act."

Brynn smiled, crossing her arms in front of her chest. "Leave that to me," she said confidently. Brynn was the bunk's resident actress—she had even acted as an extra in a major Hollywood movie last fall—and

Jenna had no doubt that her dramatic flair would lead them to an awesome, victory-ensuring act.

"Perfect," said Jenna. "Everyone think about it this morning, and we'll share ideas at our meeting this afternoon. This is *so* exciting! I mean, if I were in charge, I could . . ." She trailed off, thinking over the possibilities in her mind. Rearranging the buildings. (Well, okay, that would require major construction and possibly magic.) Stealing all the underwear at camp. (Highly entertaining, but perhaps not practical.) Planting blue dye in the shower heads, so everyone came out looking like a smurf. (*That* was a keeper.) Or . . .

"Oh my gosh!" Jenna shouted suddenly, as a vision of the Prank to End All Pranks took shape in her mind. "This could be my ticket into the *Guinness Book of World Records!*"

"*What* could be your ticket?" asked Jamie with a chuckle, suddenly stepping up behind them. "Why are you guys in such a hurry today? I've never seen kids so anxious to canoe in my life."

Jenna turned to her counselor. "Um . . . eating hot dogs," she replied, blurting out the first thing that came to mind. "I could eat, like, a ton of hot dogs tonight. But you know what, I hate hot dogs. So never mind."

She slipped away to the lake, leaving Jamie looking confused.

"Nice save," Brynn giggled, catching up to Jenna. "*Totally* smooth."

Jenna turned to her friend. "Oh my gosh, Brynn. I'm serious about this. We have to make this happen.

We *have* to win that show tonight."

Brynn just smiled, blew on her nails, and pretended to polish them on the shoulder of her shirt. "No worries, Jenna," she said simply. "We've got it in the bag."

chapter

TWO

"Oh, cool!" cried Jenna when she saw Priya step inside the tent. "That means everyone's here. Come here, Pree. I'm about to explain my plans to . . ." She looked quickly right and left, like she was afraid of being observed.

"Nobody's coming," Priya assured her. "Jasmine and Jamie are outside writing letters. I think we're safe."

Jenna nodded slowly. "The walls have ears," she murmured, which Priya thought was a supremely weird thing to say. Still, she ran over to hear Jenna's plans.

"All right," Jenna announced. "You guys, I think I could be onto something big here. *Really* big. Like history-making, legendary, getting-my-own-reality-show big."

Nat looked skeptical. "What are you talking about?" she asked.

Jenna looked around again, then moved closer to the group, gesturing to everyone to close ranks and move in closer.

"I have an idea," she said slowly, looking around at everyone's faces, "for the *biggest water-balloon fight in history.*"

Priya looked around at her friends. For a few seconds, nobody said anything. Jenna looked confused, like she didn't get why they weren't freaking out and jumping up and down.

"*Water* balloons?" asked Avery, wrinkling her nose like she'd smelled something bad. "That's it?"

"What do you mean, that's it?" Jenna asked, looking sincerely confused. "Water balloons are *awesome!*"

Priya bit her lip, feeling awkward. She knew Jenna thought water balloons were awesome—Jenna thought *anything* prank-related was awesome. And when she was in the midst of planning a good prank, Jenna could be a little . . . well . . . bossy. Priya never minded, but she knew a lot of her tentmates were tired of it.

Sarah glanced a little nervously from Avery to Jenna. "I think it could be cool," she said in a tentative voice. "Tell us more, Jenna."

Jenna nodded. "Well, David and I have had a couple of secret meetings today to work this out. At first, we had hoped to get into the *Guinness Book of World Records*, but when we saw how many balloons it would take to break the record . . . well, it seemed pretty impossible." Everyone laughed.

"Anyway," Jenna went on, looking like she didn't think it was all *that* funny, "now we're just focused on making *camp* history. We drew up a couple diagrams . . ."

She paused to pull a couple pieces of paper, folded up really tiny, from the pocket of her shorts. She unfolded them both, revealing what looked like an *incredibly* complicated battle plan from World War II or something. Different parts of the main lawn were shaded in different colors, and arrows pointed in every direction, implying, Priya guessed, different areas of attack. There were even words scrawled in the margins: "Stealthy!" and "Shoot to kill!"

Priya glanced up from the map and saw that Nat had an eyebrow raised. "How long did you and David spend on this?"

Jenna shrugged. "I dunno. A couple hours. Like six. Maybe more."

Nat crinkled up her face. "Seriously, Jenna—you don't think that's a lot of time to spend with an ex?"

Jenna looked at Nat like she was speaking Chinese. "What do you mean? We had to plan the balloon fight."

Nat sighed. "But don't you find it a little weird that David was okay with spending this much time helping his ex-girlfriend get ready for something? It's not just today, Jenna. You guys are together, like, all the time."

Jenna looked confused, but Chelsea nodded, adding, "You spend way more time together than any other ex-couple I've ever seen."

Jenna frowned, looking annoyed now. "We're *friends*. What's the big deal?"

Nat softened her tone. "Do you ever think maybe he wants to get back together with you?"

Jenna laughed—a short, sharp laugh. "Nat, seriously. Boys and girls can be *friends* without wanting to go out. Right, Priya?"

Priya nodded. She knew Jenna was referring to her longtime best-friendship with Jordan, who happened to be a boy. "Sure."

"Let's get back to the plans," Jenna concluded, tapping her finger on the map like that was the end of the conversation.

"Well . . ." Brynn said, leaning over the map, "to be honest, this looks a little complicated, Jenna."

Jenna looked surprised. "You think?"

At that moment, Sarah moved in, tracing a line of attack with her finger. "I think I get it," she said. "Avery, Nat, and I attack from the left—everyone else from the right?"

Jenna looked relieved. "That's right! And David and his bunk attack from the north and south."

Sarah nodded. "Yeah, these look like good plans to me."

Jenna grinned. "Awesome. I just wanted to let you guys in on it since you'll be super-important in helping me pull this off! David already got permission to call his cousin who lives nearby—he'll be picking up the balloons. He's going to deliver them to the main office tonight in an unmarked package, and he'll tell the staff that it's emergency underwear for David."

Brynn raised her eyebrows. "And David is okay with that? I mean, his bunk will probably tease him."

Jenna nodded. "Oh, sure. But this is more important!"

Brynn nodded, shaking her head a little and clearing her throat. "*Aaanyway*," she said, without even trying to mask the fact that she was dying to change the subject. "Shouldn't we talk about our performance?"

Everyone nodded.

Well, I thought we could do a takeoff of *America's Got Talent* and call it 'Our Bunk's Got Talent'!"

"That's a great idea," shouted Priya.

"That could be really cool! Because we could have, like, the really weird performances that are just funny, and then we could have some really good ones, too," said Sloan.

"I could dance," suggested Avery quietly, looking unusually hesitant. "I mean, I've taken ballet for years. My friends say I'm good."

Brynn nodded enthusiastically. "Perfect!" she said.

"Sloan could sing," Sarah suggested, smiling at Sloan. "Remember, you sang us that old Beatles song at campfire once, and you were so good, I got goosebumps!"

Sloan blushed. "Oh, I don't know . . ."

"I bet I could do Sharon Osbourne," Jenna suggested, a slow smile spreading over her face. She broke into a British accent. "Oh, Ozzy! Fifi's pooed on the rug again!"

"And if we want to mix in a little *American Idol*, I can *totally* do Simon Cowell," Tricia piped up, putting on a haughty British accent. "That was *dreadful*. Pointless karaoke nonsense!"

Everyone laughed at Tricia's rendition. *Who knew the president's daughter was also a gifted mimic?* As the noise level in the room rose off the charts, Brynn took a look at the faces surrounding her. Every single girl was grinning ear to ear.

"We're TOTALLY going to win this!" she shouted.

"Totally!" her friends chorused, slapping hands in a huge group high five.

That evening, everyone trooped over from dinner directly to the amphitheater. With about twenty bunks to perform, it was going to be a long night of entertainment! As soon as they arrived, all the bunks drew numbers to determine what order they would perform in. Unfortunately, Brynn had picked number twelve. Right near the end, which meant they had eleven performances to sit through. And a good, long time to get nervous.

"Oh, noooo," Jenna moaned, shaking her head and jiggling her knees in anticipation. Onstage, one of the very youngest bunks was singing a song—something about sunshine and ladybugs and believing in yourself. "You guys, I am *dying* here. Do you think we rehearsed enough? Maybe we should go rehearse again."

"Jenna," Priya said, trying to smile encouragingly. "We'll be *fine*. We rehearsed, like, a thousand times this afternoon."

"Yeah!" Tricia broke in, grinning. "And I thought we brought the house down, if I do say so myself."

"Yeah, Tricia," Avery said, "but then, you've never

been in a camp talent show before! Trust me—the competition is fierce."

Jenna moaned again.

"What she *means*," Sarah broke in, "is that everyone's at the top of their game, but we're still better. Don't worry, Jenna, we've got this in the bag."

All at once, the youngest bunk stopped singing and stood together to take their bows. The girls all clapped as Brynn turned to whisper, "That's three down, eight to go."

Jenna sighed. "Guys, this is going by *so slowly*."

"Don't worry," Priya said, trying to smile encouragingly at her bunk. "We're going to be awesome! You know we have the best skit, and we're hilarious."

A couple of her friends chimed in and tried to soothe Jenna's nerves, but the truth was, everyone seemed to be on edge. One act blended into another, and eventually Priya lost count of where they were or how long they'd been watching.

"Oh, look," Sarah said cheerfully, pointing at the stage. "David's bunk is up next."

Everyone looked up at the stage, where David and his bunkmates were lining up at the front. Priya glanced up at the familiar crew: David, Justin, Connor, Jordan, that redheaded guy, and . . . wait a minute. *Who was that?* Priya couldn't help staring at a tall, blond guy with close-cropped hair, brown eyes, and a vintage-y looking T-shirt that read WEST PHILADELPHIA TRAVELING BAND. He was about the cutest boy she'd ever seen, and she couldn't believe she'd never noticed him before. She felt warm just looking at him. Was it possible that he and she had been sharing space at Camp Walla Walla all summer? She felt her mouth hanging open, and quickly closed it.

She glanced to her right and left, but nobody else seemed as fascinated by this kid as she was. Finally she reached over and nudged Jenna.

"Hey," she hissed, as the boys onstage launched into a funny song they'd written about camp food. Jenna looked up. "Who's that?" Priya tried to gesture at the blond boy, but Jenna looked confused. "The *blond* one," Priya whispered, gesturing with her head.

Jenna looked at the stage, then back at Priya. "Ben?" she asked. "The one in the brown T-shirt?"

Priya nodded. "That's the one. How come I haven't noticed him before?"

Jenna shrugged. "He used to have this huge mop of blond curls," she explained. "Then he bet David that Dave couldn't eat twenty pancakes, but he did. So Ben had to cut off all his hair."

Priya looked back at her new crush, who was now singing a solo about meatballs. Actually . . . she *did* remember a boy about his height, always on the outskirts of David's group, with this goofy mop of golden hair, like an old-fashioned painting of an angel. She didn't remember him having such big, long-lashed, brown eyes, though. Or such a gorgeous smile.

David's bunk finished their song and everyone applauded, but Priya felt a million miles away. How long had it been since she had been this interested in a guy? A long, *long* time. So even though

Priya had never met Ben (that she remembered, anyway), and really didn't know a thing about him, she couldn't help fantasizing a little about how cool it would be to have a boyfriend at camp. "Priya!" Suddenly Jenna was shaking her shoulder, frantically gesturing toward the aisle. "Come on! Let's go!"

"What?" Priya asked, looking up at the stage. One of the sixth-grade bunks was just taking their places.

"Time to head backstage," Brynn whispered to her from her other side. "We need to take our places. We're up next!"

chapter THREE

"Omigod," Sloan moaned as she and Brynn both stared out into the packed audience. "Who knew there were *this* many kids at camp?"

"Don't worry," Brynn whispered back, "Seriously, that last rehearsal we had this afternoon was *perfect*. We've got this thing down, and there's nothing to be scared of, okay?"

Brynn turned to check in and see how Jenna was fairing, but Jenna was fine, more than fine, waving wildly at someone on the other side of the stage. Brynn followed her gaze and—sure enough, there was David, waving back and nodding. But then something else captured Brynn's attention. The boy who stood to David's left: a blond, brown-eyed guy with closely cropped hair and a cool, beat-up style T-shirt. Who *was* he? Ever since he'd sung his first line onstage, smiling and gesturing with a theatrical, even hammy air, she'd been wracking her brain. How could someone that cute have been living right under her nose all summer without her noticing him? There had to be a story. He had to be new. Or else maybe it was just that Brynn was so used to going out with Jordan, she didn't even notice other guys. No matter how cute they were. That was probably it. But now that she and Jordan had decided to call it quits earlier in the summer—no hard feelings, it just happens sometimes when two people have been together for as long as these two. They start feeling less like boyfriend and girlfriend and more like best friends—it was time to start noticing. And this guy, she definitely noticed.

Now, suddenly, the cute boy glanced up, seeming to feel her stare. Sensing a fellow extrovert, Brynn didn't look away. She smiled though somewhat tentatively. The boy smiled back and she felt the hair stand up on her arms. *Okay*, she thought to herself, trying not to do anything dorky. *Definitely some chemistry here! Now, if I can just find out what his name is . . .*

"All right, kids!" Audrey, Dr. Steve's assistant, suddenly ran over to them from her post at the edge of the stage. "The Cypress tent is almost done, and as soon as they take their bows, you're on! You'll want to line up now, and as soon as I give you the signal, get right onstage, and get started! We're running a little long tonight, and the younger kids are tired."

Brynn nodded. "Okay. We'll be ready." She signaled to her bunkmates to take their places, and after exchanging a few "OMG!" expressions, they fell into line. Brynn could almost *feel* their nervous energy behind her, but she felt so calm, she could have been relaxing in her own living room. She didn't get stage fright much anymore, but even more than that, the smile from her mystery crush had made her feel tingly all over—and made her feel like she *had* to show him her best stuff!

One of the bunks of younger boys finished singing a Jonas Brothers song and stood at the front of the stage to take their bows. As the audience applauded, Audrey coaxed the kids offstage, then waved at Brynn to move in. Brynn glanced back at her bunkmates and winked, then began confidently strolling onstage, where she and her friends quickly grabbed their props and took their places.

First up: Jenna, who took the microphone and stood at the center of the stage, mimicking the clipped tones of Sharon Osborne. "Good evening, ladies and gentlemen, and welcome to 'Our Bunk's Got Talent,' where stars are made! Tonight we've got a stellar lineup for you . . ." And before she knew it, she and her bunkmates were sailing through their act.

▲ ▲ ▲

It went *like a dream*.

It had been perfect. *She* had been perfect. And even more impressive, *everyone* onstage had been perfect! All the jokes landed perfectly, and all the serious performances were seriously applauded.

They took what felt like a hundred bows. Brynn kept waiting for the applause to die down, but it just kept coming. She could feel tears of joy building behind her eyes. She glanced at her friends, and saw that they were shiny-eyed, too. Jenna, who was on Brynn's right, reached over and grabbed her hand and gave it a squeeze. "Thanks," she whispered. "We really might win!"

Might? Brynn was about to reply when she heard a whistle from the crowd. She turned, and was drawn like a magnet to a pair of brown eyes in one of the back rows. They belonged to a guy who happened to be clapping his heart out. He whistled again, and Brynn beamed. She felt warm all over, and couldn't wait to get back in that audience so she could get more details on the cute boy with the close-cropped haircut.

Finally Audrey motioned to them to march offstage, and when they did, the applause began to quiet down. Priya skipped up near Brynn and squeezed her arm. "That was awesome, right?" she chirped, her full cheeks rosy and flushed. "We *totally* won that. Don't you think? I guess now we just have to wait it out . . ."

Brynn nodded, and a few other bunkmates piped up, weighing their chances against the best performances they'd seen that night. But Brynn was distracted. The truth was, she didn't mind waiting to find out whether they'd won—though she was *sure* they had.

After all, she had some boy research to do.

chapter

FOUR

Jenna's heart was beating a million miles a minute as she walked back into the audience to take her old seat next to David. He was grinning from ear to ear, giving her the thumbs-up every time she looked up at him. Jenna couldn't help grinning herself. She felt pretty great—like she'd just taken a ride on the world's fastest, steepest roller coaster. She still felt just as excited as she had before they'd performed, but this time it was excited-good, not excited-freaked out, like before.

"Awesome job, *compadre*," David assured her, holding up his hand for a high five as Jenna tried to squeeze by him into the row.

"Thanks mucho," Jenna replied, slapping his hand. "Although, based on my minimal Spanish, I don't think I can be a *compadre*—I think I'd have to be a *comadre*."

"Whatever," David replied, jokingly throwing up his hands. "I don't want to get into some kind of battle of the sexes with you. First of all, we've had that argument a million times, and second, I, being a boy, would totally beat you, a girl."

Jenna just sighed, glancing up at the stage. Two performances to go. Unless one of them was really a showstopper, she couldn't imagine anyone else winning the talent contest. Really, their bunk had been *incredible*. It was almost like the stars had aligned to give Jenna exactly what she wanted. Like *fate itself* wanted her to get away with the biggest prank in Camp Walla Walla history.

"Anyway," David continued, sounding a little disappointed that Jenna hadn't taken the girls-vs.-boys bait, "while you guys were performing, our counselor gave me a message. I thought you should know that *the dodo bird has landed*."

Jenna gulped. "The dodo bird has landed" was the code they had worked out this afternoon to confirm that David's cousin had delivered twenty-five bags of balloons, as planned. "I enjoy French croissants in the morning," Jenna replied, which was the code they had worked out to confirm that she would meet David in the rec room the next morning to count them. David nodded sagely, turning back to the performance onstage. But as Jenna sat back in her seat, she became aware of Priya staring at her from the other side, her eyes full of questions.

Jenna turned to her friend. "Yes?" she asked.

"What are you guys *talking about*?" Priya's face was all squished up. But Jenna knew her well enough to know she wasn't being snotty, just curious.

"What do you mean?" David asked before she could respond. "We're talking about dodo birds and

French croissants. Like there's something weird about that? What do *you* talk about?"

Priya struggled to suppress a grin. David seemed to get that response a lot. "I'll tell you what I'd *like* to talk about," she admitted, dropping her voice down to a whisper and leaning in. "That kid in your bunk, the blond . . ."

"Ben?" David asked loudly. Almost loud enough for Ben, who was sitting just a few rows away watching the show, to hear him.

Priya flinched and ducked, like she was trying to drop out of frame or something. Jenna smiled. Though Ben apparently hadn't heard them because he was still watching the show, oblivious.

"Shhhhhh!" Priya hissed to David. "Keep your voice down! I don't want him to think I *like* him or something."

Now it was Jenna's turn to stifle a grin. *Come on.* Priya was about as subtle as a herd of elephants— *obviously* she liked him.

"Oh, of course you don't like him," David replied, his voice totally deadpan. "I guess you're just asking questions about him because you're working for the Camp Walla Walla Census Bureau, or something?"

Priya blushed bright red. "Shut *up*," she begged, shaking her head as she turned back to the show. "If I can't count on you, *as a longtime friend*, to give me some confidential info . . ."

"Priya," Sarah suddenly spoke up from the seat on the other side of Priya. "Maybe you should just ask him what you want to know. The direct approach works best with David. Trust me."

Jenna took a breath. The bunk of sixth-graders onstage was finishing up and taking their bows. Just one more act . . . just *one* more . . . and she might be on her way to camp history!

David, Priya, and Sarah were still chatting, but Jenna barely heard a word they said as the next bunk—younger kids again, third-graders—came up to sing a common campfire song. The kids were really cute, and any other time, Jenna would have been laughing and clapping and whispering to her friends about how they couldn't *possibly* have ever looked that young themselves. But tonight, Jenna couldn't stop checking her watch, or trying to remember how many verses the song had.

"He *cannot* have been here all summer," Priya was exclaiming.

David just shrugged. "I have no reason to lie to you . . ."

"*Shhhhhh!*" Jenna hissed, as the kids onstage stopped singing and applause broke out. "That's it! They're the last act! They're going to announce the winners now!"

David, Priya, and Sarah all gulped down their nervousness as they turned from a very tense Jenna to the stage, where the third-graders hadn't even cleared out yet.

"I think we have a few minutes," Sarah whispered, leaning over to place a comforting hand on Jenna's arm. "Like, Dr. Steve will probably want to talk for awhile, and then . . ."

Jenna groaned. "I wish he would just *announce*

it already," she murmured. The more time passed between their performance and the announcement, the more nervous she got. She jiggled her leg.

"No worries, Jenna," Priya said gently, patting her friend's shoulder. "You know we're shoo-ins! Right, David?"

"Right," David agreed. He reached out, seeming to want to comfort Jenna, too, and his hand lingered awkwardly over her leg before he suddenly reached up and patted her on the head, like she was a Border collie or something.

Weird. Jenna flinched. She thought she was used to being David's friend—*just* his friend—but every once in a while these weird *moments* happened and she got all mixed up again. She shooed his hand away and sighed. "I'm *trying* to be patient. *Trying.*"

By now, Dr. Steve had walked back onstage, and the audience started applauding him like crazy.

"What did *Dr. Steve* do?" Jenna hissed, shaking her head. "Stop clapping! Let the man speak!"

The applause finally began to die down, and Dr. Steve smiled. "Well, campers," he said into the mike, "that was an *amazing* show! What a talented bunch you are."

More applause. Jenna tried to take deep breaths. She wished the audience came with some kind of "skip" button, so she could just fast-forward through the clapping and stuff and get to the announcement. Man, she missed her DVR!

"However," Dr. Steve went on, "there can only be one winner."

More applause. This time, though, Jenna felt a little twinge of nervousness in her stomach. She looked at David, and he looked back at her calmly, like: *You've got this.* Jenna tried to breathe. If David thought they were going to win, she trusted him. David knew funny.

"We've calculated your score with our patented *applause meter*," Dr. Steve went on, pausing to smile, "otherwise known as our ears."

Jenna groaned. "Lame!" She sighed, tapping her feet on the floor. *Just say it . . . just say it and let us keep planning . . . just say it . . .*

"And, the winner is . . ." began Dr. Steve, and suddenly Jenna felt like she was riding on the Dare Devil Dive at Six Flags. It was like a hole opened in the ground beneath her and she was falling, falling, without anything to grab onto. More than anything, she wanted Dr. Steve to name the winner, but she also *didn't*, because she was terrified it wouldn't be them—and *then* what? How would she pull off the biggest prank in camp history? What would they ever do with twenty-five bags of balloons?

Without thinking, she shoved her hand into David's and grabbed hard. His hand was warm and familiar, and he glanced at her, just for a second, before he wrapped his fingers around hers and gave her a little squeeze. Jenna looked at him, and something in the way he looked at her, the way the light from the setting sun hit his green eyes, reminded her of the millions of hours they'd spent together at Camp Lakeview a few summers ago, joking around and talking and holding hands and stuff. Was he looking at her like he *used* to look at her?

What did it mean?

For just a second, Nat's words echoed in her ear. *Do you ever think maybe he wants to get back together with you?* Jenna hadn't entertained the possibility, but . . .

"'Our Bunk's Got Talent'!" Dr. Steve shouted, and suddenly Jenna was being dragged up by her shoulders, and everyone was screaming and clapping and laughing—and then she was being pulled up onstage by her bunkmates.

"We did it!" Brynn cried with a big smile, punching Jenna in the arm as they ran up the aisle to the stage.

We did it, Jenna echoed in her head. Her plan was *on*.

And for the next twenty-four hours, she wasn't going to think about anything else besides water balloons!

chapter
FIVE

Priya woke up the next morning with a huge smile on her face. All night, she'd dreamed about Ben—having dinner with Ben, holding hands with Ben, chatting with Ben under the stars. She didn't know much about him yet, but in her dreams they'd had a *ton* in common. And even though Priya knew those had just been dreams, she couldn't deny that she just had a great *feeling* about this guy.

When she got into the bathroom to wash up, though, she suddenly felt confused. There was hardly anyone in there. Natalie stood at the sink, brushing her teeth, but she was still wearing her cute pink gingham pajamas. She paused, spit, and washed off her brush, then ran her hands under the water and tried to slick back her pillow-mushed hair.

"Hey, Priya," Nat greeted her. "What do you have your clothes on for? Remember, it's Opposite Day."

Priya groaned. She couldn't help it. Opposite Day was supposed to be fun, but she'd woken up with plans to dress to impress a certain boy camper. This was about the *last* day she would ever want to wear pajamas to breakfast.

Nat smiled at her. "Gee, you look disappointed," she said, a spark of understanding in her eyes. "Does that have anything to do with a certain cute boy I heard you asking questions about last night?"

Priya felt her face flush. She wasn't used to having crushes, and the idea of sharing this one felt a little scary, like it might lead to public humiliation. "Uh . . . um . . ." she stammered.

But Nat just looked sympathetic and patted her on the shoulder. "No worries, Priya," she assured her. "Jenna told me you were asking about Ben. And I think it's *awesome* you like him. You two will make such a cute couple!"

Priya smiled. She had to admit, it made her feel good that Nat had said "will": "You two *will* make such a cute couple"—almost like it was a done deal!

But then she remembered Opposite Day, and groaned. "The thing is," she told Nat, "I was going to dress all cute today, and I forgot we have to wear our pajamas for Opposite Day. *Now* what? I don't even have cute pajamas."

Nat glanced at the cubbies, where all their clothes and accessories were stored. "Hold on," she whispered, then darted around Priya to her cubby. She grabbed a couple of frilly, flowery pieces, then ran back to her friend. "Here, this is my extra set—how about you borrow these?"

Priya took the pajamas from Nat and looked them over. They were beautiful—a delicate flowered cami with eyelet lace accents, and a pair of purple silk pants. *Nat's pajamas are more fashionable than half my outfits,* she thought. But she couldn't deny that they seemed perfect for attracting boy attention, on a day when not many campers would be looking cute. "Are you sure?" she asked Nat. "You don't mind me borrowing them?"

Nat shook her head. "Come on. This is camp. What's mine is yours. Besides," she leaned in and whispered, "Priya, you never crush on anyone. You're so busy running around with Jordan, sometimes I wonder if you even *notice* other boys. I think you totally deserve to have a camp romance. And seriously, you and Ben would be great together. You should go after him."

Go after him. Priya wasn't entirely sure what that meant, but whatever it was, she almost felt ready. "Thanks, Nat."

"No problem."

Once Priya was dressed up in Nat's fancy pj's, Nat helped her create the perfect "just rolled out of bed looking amazing" hairstyle, and even helped apply some pink-tinted lip balm to "give your lips a little glow." Then she loaned Priya a pair of sparkly flip-flops—"Slippers would be too *obvious* with that ensemble," Nat warned—and a delicate pink cardigan to wear over the cami, in case she got chilly.

"Awesome." Nat grinned, looking over her handiwork. "You look like a million bucks!"

Suddenly, someone behind Priya yawned super loudly. Priya turned to find Brynn, wearing an old pair of gym shorts with a hoodie and rubbing her eyes. "Wow, look at you, Priya," Brynn muttered, taking in the full *look*. "You don't usually sleep this superfancy, do you?"

Priya bit her lip. She wasn't sure she wanted everyone to know that Nat was helping her dress up to win a boy's attention. But Nat just deflected Brynn's questions with a shrug. "I loaned Priya my pj's last night because she got toothpaste on hers," she said breezily. "It's no big."

Brynn shrugged and walked over to the sink to brush her teeth, and Nat looked over at Priya and winked.

"So," Brynn asked, after brushing her teeth and washing her face, "who's ready for spaghetti and meatballs for breakfast?"

Everyone groaned.

Spaghetti and meatballs for breakfast wasn't so bad, actually. It took some getting used to, but after the first few bites, Priya had to admit it tasted pretty good.

"It's just like any other breakfast when you break it down," Tricia explained. "You have your spaghetti, right, and that's carbs, just like pancakes. You have your meatballs, which are protein, like sausage or bacon. And then you have your sauce, which is kind of like maple syrup, except better for you because it has tomatoes instead of sugar. Ta-da! Breakfast."

Priya wasn't sure she'd be eating spaghetti and meatballs for breakfast again anytime soon, but just this once, it wasn't bad. Not bad at all.

And it *was* kind of funny to see the whole camp in their pajamas. Even the counselors and Dr. Steve had gotten into the act. Dr. Steve was wearing full-on old-fashioned pajamas, and he'd even found a "sleeping cap" like people always wore in old-time stories. He looked kind of ridiculous, but then, *everyone* looked so ridiculous, it wasn't as noticeable as it might have been.

After breakfast, Dr. Steve got up to speak. "Welcome to Opposite Day, everybody! Today up is down, black is white, breakfast is dinner, and the *campers are in charge!*"

"*Woooooohooooo!!!!*" screamed Jenna so loudly that Priya had to drop her fork and stick her fingers in her ears to keep from going deaf.

"Things are topsy-turvy today, so after breakfast, we're all going to take a little siesta. That's when I'll meet with the winning bunk to go over everyone's jobs for the day."

Priya turned around and glanced at Jenna, who was so excited she was bouncing in her seat. "This is going to be awesome, this is going to be awesome, this is going to be awesome . . ." she chanted under her breath.

Priya saw that Dr. Steve was looking right at their table. "After breakfast, will the winning bunk please head to my office? That's where we'll draw names to figure out who gets which job."

"Uh-oh," muttered Chelsea, prompting all the girls to turn and face one another.

"What's up?" asked Jasmine, poking at a meatball and looking around at all the campers. The counselors were still traveling with their bunks today, although once the campers-in-charge were in place, the counselors were supposed to sit back and behave like campers for the rest of the day—unless an emergency came up. "Are you worried about drawing names? They have to distribute the responsibilities somehow."

"I guess," murmured Avery, casting a concerned eye in Jenna's direction. Everyone knew Jenna had been expecting to get Dr. Steve's job for the day. It was the only way her Prank to End All Pranks would work.

But Jenna bit her lip and then said cheerfully, "It'll work however we do it. We'll all work *together* to get things done, right? All for one and one for all."

"All for one and one for all," Priya echoed. But secretly, she was already wondering what sort of job she might get. Something good, she hoped! Like maybe being in charge of the boys' bunks . . . or maybe just one *particular* boy . . .

"All right, campers, or should I say, counselors," Dr. Steve said with a smile. "Let Opposite Day begin! Members of the winning bunk, come talk to me— everyone else, enjoy your siesta!"

"Okay," Jenna hissed to her bunkmates as they

walked up the hill to Dr. Steve's office. "The word for the day is *cooperation*, got it? If anyone sees a way to throw the Dr. Steve job to me, please do. It'll make things easier. But no matter what, the most important thing is that we work together. Whoever gets to be Dr. Steve, I'm going to need your help to pull off the Prank to End All Pranks! Okay?"

"Okay," Priya agreed, along with most of her bunkmates. Even though she knew some were tired of Jenna's bossiness, they all knew Jenna was super-excited—maybe even bordering on obsessed—about this water-balloon fight. Priya hoped nothing would get in the way of making the fight happen.

Soon they reached Dr. Steve's office, which was located in a small cluster of cabins just a little north of the mess hall. "Well, welcome, ladies," Dr. Steve said graciously. He'd just walked up from the mess hall himself, and was sitting in the reception area with Audrey. Together, they were tearing off little pieces of paper from one big sheet, crinkling them up, and throwing them into Dr. Steve's sleeping cap, which he'd removed from his head. (Leaving some serious flyaways, Priya noted.)

"Hi, Dr. Steve," Jenna said with a grin. "Nice pajamas, by the way."

"Why, thank you, Jenna," Dr. Steve replied with a smile. "I could say the same to you."

He and Audrey ripped off a few more pieces and threw them into the hat, and then Dr. Steve looked thoughtful. "I think that's everything?" he asked Audrey.

She nodded. "Ten girls, ten jobs," she agreed cheerfully. "I just hope they're up to the challenge!"

Dr. Steve smiled, turning back to the girls. "I've known these girls for a long time," he said. "Some of them for many years before I even made the move to Camp Walla Walla. And so, girls, I know I can trust you with these important positions. We've been through a lot together, and I know *you* know that the running of a camp is no joke."

Priya nodded. It was true. She and her friends had had a lot of adventures together over the years—some fun ones and some not-so-fun ones. They'd spent enough time together in Dr. Steve's office to know that his job was super-serious.

"So I know you'll take your jobs very seriously," Dr. Steve went on, grabbing his hat and holding it out to the camper closest to him, Jenna. "Why don't you each take a piece of paper and hold on to it until everyone has chosen. Then you can all reveal your jobs at the same time. Once all the jobs have been revealed, any campers who want to trade will be able to do so. But *both* campers must be willing to trade jobs, all right? We don't want anyone stuck in a job they really don't want to do."

Dr. Steve passed around the hat and all the girls crowded around, hoping to get a chance to pick first. Except for Priya, that is, who held back She had some ideal jobs in mind, but she knew she'd be okay with whatever she was assigned. The most important thing for today was to make time to seek out Ben and talk to him.

Finally the hat came to Priya, and she grabbed a

paper, then passed it onto Sloan and Sarah, the only two people who hadn't chosen yet. Finally they all held their jobs in their hands.

"Okay," said Dr. Steve. "Let's go in the order you picked. Jenna, what is your job?"

Eagerly, Jenna unfolded the paper in her hand and read, "Counselor for 3rd and 4th-level bunks."

Jenna's face fell immediately, and some of the campers exchanged concerned looks. Jenna was supposed to be in charge of the youngest campers—a *huge* job, and one that would take a lot of concentration. It was hard to imagine Jenna looking after the youngest kids and still having time to pull off the Prank to End All Pranks.

Avery and Chelsea read theirs next—they were the Arts and Crafts Supervisor and the Mess Hall Supervisor, respectively. The next person to read her job was Brynn. She unfolded her paper and beamed. "Head of Camp Operations," she read.

Brynn was Dr. Steve for the day!

Priya looked right to Jenna, who seemed to be shooting darts with her eyes at Brynn. Every muscle and body part seemed to be begging, *"Give it to me, give it to me, give the Dr. Steve job to me!"* Priya almost hoped it wasn't as obvious to Dr. Steve and Audrey as it seemed to her. Especially because Brynn didn't seem to notice Jenna at all. She smiled down at her piece of paper, like she was already thinking about fun things she could do with her new position.

"*A-hem.*" Jenna cleared her throat very loudly, and Brynn shook her head.

"Oh, sorry!" Brynn looked up and smiled at everyone, then turned to Natalie. "Go ahead, Nat."

Jenna's mouth dropped open, like she couldn't believe this was happening, and right at that moment, Brynn looked right at Jenna and gave her the thumbs-up, with a wink. Jenna looked stunned, but then something seemed to click in her head.

Okay, Priya thought, *so Brynn isn't going to give her the Dr. Steve job, but she'll help? I guess?* Maybe that was just as good? But how would Jenna ever get out of watching the little kids?

"Hey, Priya!" Someone yanked on Priya's ponytail to get her attention, and Priya turned to face Sarah and the rest of her bunk. She'd spaced out for a minute there, watching the mini-drama between Jenna and Brynn. "Time to read your job!"

Priya glanced down at the nearly-forgotten paper in her hand. "Oh!" She unfurled it, and read in a loud voice: "Counselor for the upper level campers!"

The upper level campers. That was them—their age level, and one grade below! Priya realized she was in charge of the oldest kids at camp. It was an insanely easy job, or at least she thought it would be; kids their age already knew the ins and outs of camp and didn't get in much trouble, aside from pulling pranks, of course. Plus, Priya was basically getting the ability to boss around her closest friends and the boys their age! She smiled, realizing that she would have the power to pull Ben out of his activities for a little one-on-one . . . this would be the perfect opportunity to get to know him better!

"*A-hem.*" Priya shook out of her daydream in time to see Jenna holding up her paper and clearing her throat. "*I* would like to trade jobs, if anyone's interested." She looked around the room. Nobody spoke up, at least not right away. It seemed like everyone was more or less happy with their assignments—Sloan was Nature Supervisor, Nat was in charge of the middle school kids, and Sarah was the Athletics Supervisor. Tricia was in charge of Special Activities, and she was already scribbling ideas on her hand with a pen she'd grabbed from Dr. Steve's desk. It was a little crazy how perfectly suited for their job everyone seemed to be.

As the seconds ticked by, Priya could see Jenna's eyes widening, and she started to feel a little nervous herself. Was it possible that, right after their "teamwork" pep talk, no one was going to help Jenna out? When it came right down to it, was everyone too sick of "bossy Jenna" to help with the water-balloon fight? Priya had to wonder. Everyone loved Jenna, of course, but sometimes she *could* get a little crazy over her pranks. Maybe no one wanted to feel pressured to give up a position they were going to love.

The words were out of Priya's mouth before she even had a chance to think about them. "I'll do it!"

Jenna turned to her, relief washing over her face. "Um—are you sure?" she asked, looking like she desperately wanted Priya to be sure.

"Sure," Priya insisted, before considering the question. *Was* she sure? She was giving up the easiest job of the day for, arguably, the hardest. And if she was going to spend the whole day chasing seven- and eight-year-olds, there was *no way* she'd get to spend any time with Ben. Which kind of stunk.

Jenna looked at Priya like she'd just announced that yes, Chace Crawford would love to take her to the prom. She ran forward and threw her arms around Priya. "*Thank you*, Priya, omigod." She pulled away and looked around awkwardly, seeming to realize how that must have looked to Dr. Steve. "I mean—I'm no good with little kids. All that crying and puking. You know."

"Sure," muttered Priya, although Jenna was freaking her out a little. *Crying and puking?* The crying she could handle, but . . .

"Great, girls," Dr. Steve announced with a big smile. "I'm glad you've worked this all out. And just in time! Because my official duties end . . . right *now!*" He grabbed his sleeping cap from Audrey and plopped it back on top of his head. "Starting at this moment, I'm just a humble camper. I'm going to move from bunk to bunk, trying to get the full Camp Walla Walla experience. Girls, please feel free to come find me, or any of the counselors, if you feel like you're in over your head. Don't hesitate. We'd be much happier to help you deal with a situation as it happens than to have to help you pick up the pieces when something goes wrong. Understand?"

Priya's bunkmates all glanced at one another and slowly nodded. "We understand."

"Great." Dr. Steve smiled again, adjusted his cap, and strode toward the door. "I guess I'm off for my siesta, then! Our morning campfire starts in half an hour, girls—you'll take over then. You may have the next thirty minutes to lay out plans. Remember—a strict schedule is crucial when you're working with lots of kids! If you lose control even for a second, they'll turn against you."

Priya gulped. The last thing she wanted was forty or fifty third-graders turned against her. She was worried enough about the crying and the puking.

Brynn stepped out into the mid-morning sunshine with a huge smile on her face. She was *in charge!* She hadn't even really wanted the Dr. Steve job, but when she'd opened up that little piece of paper, she couldn't deny that her heart had *soared*. Brynn was used to directing people onstage—telling them where to go, where to stand, how to sing, and what expressions to make. In real life, though, she often felt like a supporting player to some of the stronger personalities in her bunk. This was her big chance to wield real power! Plus, she deserved it—the skit had been her idea, and she'd directed her friends to give a perfect performance.

And—she couldn't deny it even to herself—she was hoping maybe now she'd have some free time to spend with the boy from the talent show. After their performance last night, she'd gone over and introduced herself. They hadn't talked much, but she felt a little spark between them.

"All right," Jenna announced, as soon as they were out on the lawn and out of Audrey's earshot. (She wasn't technically in charge today, sure, but they had no doubt she'd report them if she caught wind of the Prank to End All Pranks.) "So, *Brynn*, you seemed kind of preoccupied in there, but you're still on board to help with tip-teep, right?"

Brynn frowned. *Preoccupied? And*—"Tip-teep?" she asked, puzzled.

"The Prank to End All Pranks," Jenna explained, looking a little exasperated. "T.P.T.E.A.P. Tip-teep."

"Oh." Brynn tried to let that sink in. "Okay. Yeah, sure, of course I'm on board."

"I just couldn't help but *notice*," Jenna went on, looking at Brynn intensely, "that you didn't seem to see my signals to throw me the Dr. Steve job in there."

Brynn looked at Jenna. Had she ignored her friend's signals in there? Well, not exactly. It had never occurred to her to thwart Jenna's plans, or to avoid helping her friend. But in truth, when she had opened her little sheet of paper and seen Dr. Steve's job, she had been so excited for a minute that she maybe-on-purpose avoided looking at *anyone*. Was that so wrong? To just want to enjoy her good fortune, and let everyone else deal for a minute?

Besides, did Jenna really *need* Dr. Steve's job?

"I'm sorry if I worried you," Brynn said honestly. "But I think we can still make tip-teep happen! With you in charge of the older campers, you'll have lots of free time to prepare—and you can yank whoever you need out of their activities to help you."

Jenna nodded. "True," she agreed, and looked away, seemingly satisfied with the whole situation.

"Anyway, preparations are *way* necessary—like, we need to start filling balloons ASAP. I'll grab David out of his tent, but I'll need all of you to help at some point, too."

"No problem," said Priya.

"Sure," agreed Sarah.

"Yeah, I'll *totally* help," Tricia added. "This will be my first camp prank!"

Jenna smiled. "Tricia," she said, "I think it would make the most sense to have the water-balloon fight right after dinner—er, breakfast. That way we can store the balloons in the mess hall and get everybody involved. As the Special Activities Coordinator, maybe you can come up with some exciting activity for right after dinner that everyone can be heading to when the fight breaks out."

Tricia grinned. "Word, chica! Consider it done. Maybe a nice, peaceful bird-watching hike?"

Sloan nodded. "That's totally upside down," she said, "because most birds come out in the morning, not at night."

Jenna nodded, getting a faraway look in her eyes like she was trying to think of anything she missed. "Right after campfire, David and I will move the balloons from his tent to the mess hall," she said. "We'll fill them up there, in the faculty bathroom so no one sees. Is that okay with you, Chelsea?"

Chelsea shrugged. "Sure. I'll just tell the staff it's Opposite Day, so they should use the campers' restrooms."

"Okay," Jenna said, nodding and biting her lip, like

she was still feeling stressed. Brynn had a feeling her friend was going to be a ball of nerves all day—until the balloon fight happened, anyway. Meanwhile, the more Brynn thought about the fight—T.P.T.E.A.P., as Jenna called it—the less exciting it seemed. Although, if she could somehow corner her crush . . . *then* the water-balloon fight might get exciting . . .

As Brynn's mind wandered, she suddenly noticed a familiar, golden-haired figure walking across the lawn toward the buildings that housed Dr. Steve's office and a handful of other camp services. Speak of the devil! He looked so adorable, Brynn almost wondered whether he was a mirage. Could she really be so lucky? Was her crush just *loping toward her* out of nowhere, when he should be taking siesta with the rest of his bunk?

Just then, the mirage smiled a slow, easy smile and called to Brynn. "Hey, you!"

Brynn felt her face growing hot. She couldn't keep a huge smile from spreading over her face. "Hey," she called back. "What are you doing over here?"

He sighed. "Would you believe I fell off my bed?" he asked, shaking his head like he couldn't believe it. "It could only happen to me, man. I was trying to get comfortable and *slam!* At least I sleep on the bottom."

Brynn chuckled. "Um, that's a shame, but it doesn't explain what you're doing here."

He grinned. "I'm headed to the nurse's office," he explained, holding up his scraped elbow. "For a Band-Aid. It *really* hurts. Do you want to kiss it and make it better?"

Brynn had no idea what to say to that, so she

started laughing. He chuckled, too, seeming to enjoy the fact that he'd left her speechless, and loped away toward the nurse. "Later!" he called.

Brynn just smiled. In her head, she was already picturing the two of them at the water-balloon fight. If this boy could crack her up using only a scraped elbow as a prop, she couldn't even imagine how funny he'd be in the heat of a water-balloon battle. She could go after him really hard, just to show him she wasn't to be messed with . . . and once the fight was over, maybe they could wander over by the lake, since, as Head of Camp Operations, she didn't really have anywhere she needed to be . . .

"Earth to Brynn!" Nat's shriek brought Brynn racing back to the present, where she blinked and realized that, yeah, her entire bunk was staring at her. *Oops!*

"Yeah?" she asked, feeling a little sheepish.

Nat shook her head, an "I can't believe you" expression on her face. "I *said*, what was *that* all about?"

Brynn swallowed. Had she been that obvious? "Um . . . all of what?"

Avery rolled her eyes. *"Hello,"* she replied. "That *boy*. You were so into him, I thought you were going to carry him to the nurse's office yourself."

Tricia nodded, letting out a little chuckle. "Yeah," she said. "I mean, I've been going to an all-girls school since I was six, and even *I* could tell there was something going on there. Spill!"

Brynn felt herself blushing again. Well, she rarely kept secrets from her friends—and there was no reason to hide her feelings. "Okay, maybe I have a little crush," she admitted.

"On *him?*" Priya asked. She looked upset for some reason, which was weird—Priya was the most happy-go-lucky camper in the bunk. It took a natural disaster to upset her. Even then, she could probably find a bright side to a hurricane.

Brynn shrugged. Maybe Priya had gotten up on the wrong side of the bed this morning—though she did look *adorable* in her supercute pajamas. "Yeah, him," Brynn confirmed cheerfully. "I guess he's been at camp all this time, but he just cut his hair or something? Anyway, I think he's *so* cute. And I talked to him after the show last night, and I think we have a lot in common."

A few of the girls smiled at Brynn—Chelsea even let out a little, *"ooooh, Brynn's got a new crush"*—but weirdly enough, Priya only looked more upset. And actually—*Natalie* was kind of glaring at her, too. What had she ever done to *Nat*, she wondered?

"Brynn," Nat said finally, her mouth still drawn in a tight line, "are you talking about Ben? The Ben who's in David's bunk?"

"Yeah," Brynn said cheerfully, looking after him, toward the nurse's office. "That's him! He said he used to have really curly hair?"

Priya gulped. Brynn turned back around in time to see her and Nat exchange a serious look.

"Brynn," Nat said gravely, "there's something you should know."

"What?" asked Brynn. Her mind was spinning

through a million plots from the soap operas she loved to DVR and watch when she came home from school. Was Ben in the mafia? Did he have only months to live? Was he—oh, God—"Is he my cousin or something?"

"Worse," said Natalie, her expression still serious.

Worse? Brynn wondered. "Is he a serial killer? Is he the guy who ran over my puppy when I was six?" *Wait, that's not possible. If I was six, he would have been six, too. Or seven, if he had a birthday in the fall. Way too young to drive a car . . .*

"The thing is," Priya was saying, seeming to have trouble getting the words out, "I like him, too."

Brynn was so busy running through the possibilities in her head, she almost didn't hear Priya at first. And when she did, it took her a minute to process the words.

So Priya liked Ben, too.

That was all?

"I'm sorry," Brynn said automatically, though, as she thought about it, she really did feel sorry for her friend. "It's just, he was so funny, goofing around with his friends, and I guess that caught my eye . . ."

Priya nodded. "That's what I noticed, too. I mean, that, and . . . well . . . I don't know. I just looked at him onstage, and it was like he was looking right at me. I just felt this *connection* to him."

Brynn smiled. "Yeah, that's how I felt."

Everyone was quiet for a minute.

"So what do we do?" asked Priya finally. Her voice sounded kind of sad, like she already knew the answer and didn't like it.

"I guess . . ." Brynn started, but she was cut off by Natalie.

"Brynn," Nat said forcefully, suddenly all business, "when did you first notice Ben?"

Brynn thought about it. "When we were standing backstage waiting to go on. I mean, I caught the end of their performance, but then when he was just fooling around with the guys, I kind of couldn't stop staring." She paused. "And I felt him looking at me when we did our skit. That might sound lame, but it's totally true."

Nat nodded, not showing any other outward reaction. "Okay," she said crisply. "Priya, when did *you* notice him?"

Priya looked from Nat to Brynn and back again, confused.

"Priya," Nat coaxed, "just answer the question."

Priya gulped. "Well," she said, "it was like I said, when he first went onstage. It was like my eyes were magnets and he was, like, a refrigerator door."

Avery snorted. "*Lovely* imagery there, Priya."

Priya ignored Avery's comment. "Anyway," she went on, "I asked Jenna about him, because she was sitting right there."

Jenna looked up from the notes she was doodling, as if she was noticing this conversation for the first time. "That's right," she confirmed. "Priya thought he was new or something. But I said no, he just cut his hair."

Priya nodded. "Right," she agreed. "So then . . . I don't know. I just got interested, I guess. I was asking David about him later. I thought I'd try to talk to him today."

Brynn bit her lip. This was all very interesting and unfortunate, but in her mind, facts were facts. "Well," she said, "I'm sorry, but I didn't know anything was going on and I kind of talked to him last night." She paused, and when nobody said anything, she added, "I think we're kind of, like . . . in the pre-stages. You know, we have a lot in common."

Nat cocked an eyebrow. "Did he ask you out?"

"No," Brynn admitted, "but—"

Avery looked skeptical. "Did you guys talk about going out, at all?"

"Yeah," Chelsea jumped in. "Or did he, like, ask if you had a boyfriend or anything?"

Brynn scowled. She could feel this conversation spinning out of control. "No," she admitted. "But that's only because it was obv—"

"Hmmmm," said Nat. That was all she said, just "hmm," but her meaning was clear. Brynn usually loved Nat, but right now she wanted to scream. This was so simple. She and Priya both liked Ben, okay—but it seemed like Ben liked *her* back. Why was Nat trying to turn this into a court trial?

"Priya," Sloan spoke up suddenly, giving her friend a concerned look, "do you still like Ben? Would you still, like, want a chance to talk to him? Or do you think it's a lost cause?"

Priya looked surprised. "No," she insisted. "It's not a lost cause. We never even really got a chance to talk. Of *course* I want a chance with him."

Brynn wanted to shout *Too late, too late,* but she bit her lip. She knew Priya hadn't done anything wrong, and she was just being honest about how she felt. But still, this whole conversation didn't seem fair. Why was everyone so concerned with *Priya's* feelings—not Ben's?

Suddenly Tricia, who'd been watching the whole thing with wide eyes, like she was watching exotic animals at the zoo, spoke up. "It kind of seems like Priya had dibs," she said.

"*Dibs?*" Brynn spouted, before she could stop herself.

Tricia nodded. "Sure," she said. "You know, like when you get to ride shotgun because you say 'shotgun' before anyone else." She paused. "Isn't that how it works?"

"This isn't *shotgun,*" Brynn replied, but everyone else was talking at the same time.

"I kind of agree," Nat was saying, turning to Brynn with a serious expression. "Look, Brynn—you have a new crush every day of the week. But Priya's only fallen for this one guy in like, months. If Priya gets to know him, you'll find a new guy in no time. But if you start going out with him . . ." She trailed off, but her meaning was clear. *Priya dies miserable and alone, all because you took her camp boyfriend. Could you live with that?*

"It's only fair," Avery agreed, looking pensive. "I mean, I would like to think our friendships with each other are more important than some stupid *boy.*"

"Right," Sarah agreed, sounding a little nervous. "I'd rather have you guys as friends than, like, any guy."

Avery nodded, walking over to Brynn and putting her hand on her shoulder. "Really, Brynn—wouldn't you rather have Priya's friendship than some silly fling with—what'shisname?"

"Ben," Brynn replied at the same time as Priya.

Avery wore a sugary smile. "We girls have to stick together—don't you agree?"

"Sure," agreed Brynn, her heart beating quickly. "But—"

"Then you'll do what's fair," Avery finished, cutting Brynn off. "Since Priya noticed him first, she gets the first chance to get to know him. If it doesn't work out, then you can try your luck."

Brynn didn't know what to say. She'd been trying and trying to argue her point, but now that everyone else was finally silent, she felt beaten. If their friendship was more important than boys, then shouldn't it be able to weather these petty differences over whose crush beat whose?

Nat straightened up from the tree she'd been leaning on and turned to Priya. "Is that okay with you, Priya?"

Priya blinked. She seemed as stunned by all this as Brynn felt—though, understandably, not as angry. "Sure," she whispered, then cleared her throat. "I mean, I guess," she continued, more loudly. "I guess—I'll just try to talk to him today, then."

"Great." Nat smiled. She turned to Brynn, and Brynn could tell that her friend didn't get it—she had no idea that she'd upset Brynn at all. "We'll let Priya have a chance, then. Oh my gosh!" She glanced at her watch. "We have, like, five minutes till the campfire. We should all get going."

Slowly, and with lots of conversation, all of Brynn's friends got to their feet and started moving. Brynn felt frozen in place, though. She glanced over at the nurse's building: still no sign of Ben.

"Brynn?" called Priya, looking back with wide, hopeful eyes. "You're coming, right?"

Brynn looked at her friends, already arranged in little clumps, ready to head off to the campfire. She clutched the little piece of paper she'd shoved in her pocket, the one that read HEAD OF CAMP OPERATIONS. She didn't *have* to go to the campfire. She didn't *have* to do anything today.

"You know what?" she asked, smiling weakly. "I think I'll just stay here. Get the lay of the land."

Priya looked disappointed, but Nat grabbed her hand. "Come on, guys. We don't want to be late to our first activity where we're in charge."

Priya took Nat's hand, and slowly, Brynn watched her friends disappear across the lawn toward the campfire pit. After a few minutes, she walked back inside Dr. Steve's office, through the reception area, and over to Dr. Steve's desk. She dropped into Dr. Steve's comfy office chair, letting her eyes wander out the window to the building that housed the nurse's office.

She would play by the rules. She'd be the good friend, like always—she'd let Priya have her shot at Ben. She'd see whether they hit it off.

But today, Brynn thought, twirling cheerfully in her chair, *I have the last word*.

SEVEN

"We're going to do this assembly-line-style," Jenna announced, tearing into a bag of balloons and pulling out a handful. "Chelsea, you will hand the balloons to me, one by one, by the opening, okay?"

Jenna handed a balloon to Chelsea, rubbery tip first. That way Chelsea could easily fit it around the faucet and fill it right away.

"Okay," Chelsea agreed, looking a little bored. "How long am I on this, again?"

Jenna sighed. "As long as it takes," she replied. And looking around at the hundreds of balloons that surrounded them, this was looking more and more like an all-day activity. Luckily, though, she'd managed to get away from her "official" camp duties with no problem whatsoever, telling Crystal—the actual, non–Opposite-Day supervisor for the oldest kids—that she and David were working on an "independent study." Once Chelsea had instructed the kitchen staff on what to make for lunch, she'd been able to join them, too. The three of them were crowded a little too close in the faculty bathroom, the door closed to keep any of the kitchen staff from seeing what they were really up to. Things were a bit cozy inside, but hey, Jenna figured, they were all friends.

"Then," Jenna went on, taking the balloon back from Chelsea, "I will fill up said balloon." She took the balloon and stretched the mouth around the sides of the faucet, then turned on the water. *Glub, glub, glub,* and the balloon was filled. "You want to get them nice and full," Jenna instructed her friends. "I mean, if you guys take over when I take a break or something. Okay? Nice and full. We want people to get *soaked* when one of these babies hits them." She paused, carefully removing the balloon from the faucet, and then held it out to David, cradling the globe of the balloon in one hand and the opening in the other.

"*Then,*" Jenna went on, "David will tie off the balloon and put it in one of these garbage bags." David reached out to take the balloon from Jenna, and as soon as she removed her hands, *Gloosh!* It rolled over in his hand, spilling water all over his shorts and T-shirt.

"David!" Jenna squealed. This was no time for playing around.

"Calm down, General Patton," David urged, holding out a hand to fend her off as he dropped the near-empty balloon in the sink and grabbed some paper towels. "It's *your* fault for overfilling the balloon. Go a little easier next time."

Jenna looked at him, tensing her jaw. "This is really *important,* David," she stressed.

"I know," David said. He looked her in the eye, unfazed. Jenna felt herself relax a little. She and David had pulled many pranks together before—so if he thought there was nothing to worry about, then maybe there really wasn't anything to worry about.

"Okay. Let's get started," Jenna said with a new resolve. She turned back to Chelsea, who actually looked a little nervous as she pulled the first balloon out of the bag and handed it to Jenna, opening first, as instructed.

"Let's *do* this!" cried David in a gruff voice as Jenna stretched the balloon over the faucet and turned the water on.

Jenna couldn't help it. She smiled.

Maybe T.P.T.E.A.P. really would go off as planned—and she would become a camp legend!

▲ ▲ ▲

About an hour later, Chelsea, David, and Jenna found themselves standing in the door to the mess hall as it filled up with hungry campers. Everyone was still in their pajamas, and they seemed especially keyed-up after a morning of quiet "evening" activities, like campfire and siesta. Chelsea was smiling, no doubt anticipating the reaction to her new meal arrangements. As more and more campers approached, Chelsea quickly spoke to the mess hall manager, George, and then strode up to the same microphone where Dr. Steve had made his Opposite Day announcement the morning before.

"Welcome to the *new* mess hall!" Chelsea announced cheerfully. "This is Opposite Day, so I want to shake things up a little. Effective immediately, bunks do *not* have to sit together! Everyone can sit wherever they want—even if it's with friends from another bunk, or even another division!"

"This should be interesting," David muttered to Jenna, wiping his wet hands on his jeans. Jenna nodded.

Chelsea went on: "Second, on Opposite Day, the counselors and CITs can rest up! Effective today only, the *youngest person* at each table will serve the group. Okay, everybody—find your seats!"

As soon as Chelsea put down the microphone, total chaos broke out. Kids were scrambling everywhere, pushing and fighting to claim a table, any table. And soon, the air was filled with voices shouting for their friends: "KYLE!", "GINA!", "JENNA AND DAVID, OVER HERE!"

Jenna looked up. She'd been so amazed by the hectic scene, she'd forgotten that she was going to have to find a seat in this mess, too. So she was relieved when she saw Chelsea commandeering a table near the kitchen and calling over to her and David. Nat was already pulling out a chair to sit down. And Jenna could see Nat calling to Priya—and, soon after, to Ben.

Jenna couldn't help but smile. *Let the matchmaking begin.*

She started walking toward the table, and was a little startled when David followed her. Not that she didn't like spending time with David, obviously, but— she looked at Nat, innocently chatting with Priya, and gulped. Nat had been right the other morning. David *was* acting almost . . . clingy lately. It was weird. It was unlike him.

It made Jenna think he had a reason.

"Where do you think you're going?" she asked, turning to face David when they were just a few feet away from the table.

David looked confused. "Um . . . to sit down?"

"You're sitting with us?" Jenna demanded, letting an icy tone slip into her voice.

"Yeah." David was looking at her like she had nine heads, all of them crazy. "Is that weird or something?"

Jenna sighed, catching Nat's eye. Nat raised an eyebrow, and Jenna could tell what she was thinking—*See? He can't stand to be away from you.* She bit her lip, then spat, "The thing is, we spent practically all morning together, and most of yesterday afternoon, too. Don't you have any other friends?"

The minute the words were out of her mouth, she regretted them. They were too harsh, too mean. She wanted to know what David was up to, but she hadn't meant to sound *cruel* like that.

But David just snorted. "Well, you know how it is," he replied, lifting his arm over his head and sniffing his armpit. "I kind of smell from all that balloon-filling-up. I wouldn't want to stink up the table of people I actually like!"

Jenna heard her friends at the table laughing. She should have known. David never took anything seriously. It was the most awesome and most aggravating thing about him. "Never mind," she said with a sigh, sinking into a chair.

"It's okay, David," Sarah said encouragingly, grabbing a chair on the other side of Jenna. "As long as you sit downwind, you're welcome to join us."

David grinned. "Same to you."

Sarah shrugged. "Not necessary," she replied. "I showered twice this morning."

Nat cleared her throat, looking across the table at Priya and Ben. *"Anyway,"* she said, casting a glance at David that clearly meant *cool it.* "None of my favorite TV shows are on during the summer. What are *your* favorite shows, Ben?"

Ben looked thoughtful. "I like *Top Gear,*" he said after a moment, smiling at Nat. "It's on BBC America. And I love to watch Comedy Central—I love stand-up comedy."

"Me too, dude," David said, leaning his head out over the table to look down at Ben. "I'd almost like to try it someday, but I think I'd be too nervous."

"Totally," Ben agreed, smiling. "It's not like acting. It's like you're playing *yourself.* If nobody laughed, I'd freak out."

Nat cleared her throat. *"Priya* went to a comedy club last spring, didn't you, Priya?"

Priya, who'd been staring at Ben like she couldn't believe he was right next to her, looked at Nat, momentarily confused. "Oh, right," she said finally. "My friend had a birthday party there. They do like this pizza and soda party thing in the afternoon for kids. It was fun."

"Cool, man," Ben said, turning his smile to her. "I

wish they had something like that where I live. I watch Comedy Central all the time, but that's not nearly as cool as going to an actual club. That's awesome."

Suddenly Jenna became aware of a disturbance brewing on the other side of the mess hall. She turned around, and spotted a gaggle of fifth-grade boys shouting at each other, seemingly over an empty seat at the table. Natalie, who was in charge of the middle campers, stood up, and Chelsea watched for a moment before they both rushed over to the scene. From a table in another corner, Dr. Steve, still in his silly pajamas and cap, leaped to his feet and also walked over.

Chelsea tried her hardest to soothe the younger boys, but they were too angry and upset. It wasn't until Dr. Steve reached the little group that the shouting stopped. Seeing Dr. Steve seemed to remind some of the *other* campers of how unhappy they were with this new seating arrangement though, because suddenly other campers started running over to the area, all shouting, "Dr. Steve, Dr. Steve!"

Jenna shook her head and turned back to her friends at the table.

"Maybe choose-your-own-table wasn't such a good idea," David suggested.

"Speaking of which," Ben added, "other tables are eating already. Who's the youngest at our table? I'm starving."

After some quick calculations, they figured out that Sarah was the youngest, and therefore responsible for serving everyone. Well, she was the youngest aside from Nat and Chelsea—but everyone was really too hungry to wait for them.

Sarah got up to get the food, but already, Jenna was hearing moans and complaints from campers around them.

"It's sticky!" one young girl moaned.

"It's too sweet," complained a middle school boy. "It's like eating dessert for lunch. Kind of gross."

Jenna frowned. "What's for lunch?" she asked David, wondering if Chelsea had mentioned it to him while they were filling up balloons. It hadn't occurred to her to ask.

David made a face. "Salmon burgers," he replied.

Ew. Jenna didn't want to complain and seem disloyal to her friend, but yeah—that was an odd choice. Lots of kids at Camp Walla Walla didn't even like seafood, never mind a fishburger.

Jenna was beginning to wish she'd eaten more spaghetti this morning. She could only hope there'd be something more appealing for dinner—pancakes maybe? That was opposite, for sure.

"Look," said Connor, pointing to the spot where Chelsea, Natalie, and Dr. Steve were still talking down disgruntled campers. "Here comes Brynn!"

Jenna followed his gaze. Sure enough, there was their friend, getting up from the table she shared with Tricia, Sloan, and Avery to run over to the angry group.

"Looks like this little experiment in mess hall seating didn't work out," Jenna observed. Just then, Sarah returned with the first round of plates, and stuck a steaming salmon burger in front of Jenna. Jenna breathed in the fishy aroma—*yuck*—and sighed.

After a few minutes, Brynn stepped up to the microphone to make an announcement.

"Campers," she said agreeably, "maybe this new seating arrangement isn't working for you. It seems some tables just don't have enough seats to fit all our friends, and maybe sitting together with our bunks is a *good* thing—at least, for most of us."

Little grunts of agreement sounded all over the mess hall. Jenna was surprised—but she supposed it made sense. Having to think about where they would sit just gave campers an excuse to split up and fight, and Jenna had to admit, she was already sort of wondering what was up with the other half of their bunk. What was she missing by sitting at the table Brynn had chosen?

"We'll go back to sitting by bunk tomorrow," Brynn promised. Behind her, Chelsea looked sheepish. Jenna could tell her friend was embarrassed by how badly her ideas were going over so far. "In the meantime," Brynn went on, "we'll keep these same tables for dinner, to cut down on confusion. And I have an announcement that I think will cheer you up."

The mess hall went quiet. Jenna supposed everyone was super-curious to hear Brynn's new plan.

"It's Opposite Day," Brynn went on, "and to me, that means doing the *opposite* of what we usually do at camp. And what do we usually have in the afternoon?"

There was a cacophony of voices. "Sports!" someone yelled. While another cried, "Swimming," and another, "Crafts!" The truth was, campers usually spent the afternoon in rotating activities. According to the regular schedule, Jenna would have had sports, siesta, and swimming, in that order.

"The answer," Brynn replied, speaking up to be heard over the shouting of the campers, "is *organized activities!* And I think we all need a break, don't you? So this afternoon, for the first time, I'd like to announce that all activities are canceled! You can do whatever you like—whether it is swimming, hiking, or nothing at all!"

The mess hall was quiet for just a second. Then it erupted in cheers. Jenna knew that her afternoon activities were set—no matter what, she was filling up water balloons. But still, she had to admit that Brynn's idea was kind of genius. An afternoon to do *anything* sounded amazing—and, yeah, totally un-camp-like. Brynn had totally won back the crowd. Jenna was impressed.

"Okay," Brynn continued, shouting again even as the cheering died down, "I'm happy you're all happy! I'm working on adding some new optional activities for those who want to leave camp grounds, or try something different. I'll announce them later, though. For now, enjoy your meal!"

Brynn left the microphone and headed toward Nat and Chelsea. After a brief chat, Nat and Chelsea headed back to their table. Jenna turned back to her "lunch." This fishburger, though, was *so* not her thing. But she was starving, so she decided to get up and fix herself a peanut butter and jelly sandwich at the "emergency" table set against the wall. The table was always there and always amply stocked with bread, peanut butter, and jelly for campers who were violently opposed to whatever was being served that day.

It was clear from the mob around the table that Chelsea's salmon burgers were not going over well. Jenna had to wait about ten minutes to even get her supplies together, and then she was crowded on all sides by other campers doing exactly what she was doing.

"We're wasting so much food," Jenna overheard one kitchen staffer whispering to the other. "I tried to tell her. Kids are picky. Best to stick to the tried and true."

The other staffer just gazed over at the PB&J table, looking concerned. "I hope we don't run out of bread."

Finally armed with her sandwich, Jenna headed back to the table, taking a huge bite along the way. When she got back, she was met by uproarious laughter. Everyone was cracking up, and from the pleased look on David's face, she could tell it was from something he'd said.

"So then," David went on, "I said to her, 'Look, if this is your idea of a swanky dinner, I'd love to take you out for a four-course meal at Mickey D's.'"

Jenna wrinkled her nose. She knew this story. "Are you talking about your cousin, again?" she asked, sitting down.

David glanced at her and shrugged. "Maybe I am, Jens. You can't be the only person I impress with my comic genius."

Jenna stifled a groan, taking another huge bite of her sandwich.

Nat, looking none too pleased with this conversational detour, leaned across the table toward Priya and Ben. "Ben, what are your favorite foods? We know what *David's* are."

Jenna cringed. *Obvious much?* She wondered if Ben, who seemed for all intents and purposes like a cool guy, felt weird being the subject of twenty questions.

But Ben just smiled and stroked his chin. "Hmmm," he said in this exaggerated, almost theatrical way. Actually, Jenna thought, she could totally see him and Brynn getting along—they were both hams. "Well, I love Thai food."

"Interesting." Nat pasted on a slightly forced-looking smile and turned to Priya. "Priya, don't you like Thai?"

Priya, who'd been watching Ben, looked surprised. "Not really," she admitted. "But I haven't had it much. It always seems a little too sweet to me."

"Ah," said Ben, "that's because you're ordering the wrong thing. You need to go for the spicy stuff, like the curries."

Priya smiled. "I love curries!"

Nat beamed, clearly happy with her matchmaking skills, but then David interrupted.

"Did you see that YouTube video of the cat that ate curry vindaloo?" he asked.

Jenna sighed, putting down her sandwich. She had seen that video, and it was *not* appropriate lunch conversation. "David, shhhh," she hissed.

"What?" he asked, turning to her and laughing a little. "I won't go into detail. It's crazy though, because the cat gets into its owner's take-out, and . . ."

"*David!*" Jenna barked. "Stop! Seriously!" What was *with* him today? All of these jokes and stories . . . and even more than what he was saying, this goofy tone of voice he was using. He was totally acting like "On" David, the David that only came out when he was looking for attention, or really wanted to impress someone. In fact . . .

Jenna gulped.

It kind of reminded her of how he acted when they first started going out, and he was trying to impress *her*, and her friends.

As Priya and Ben chatted merrily away about all manner of multiculti cuisine, Jenna pushed her sandwich away. As hungry as she'd been, she suddenly felt like she'd lost her appetite. It almost seemed impossible to deny now. David was hanging around her every second of the day, he was helping her with the balloon prank, and he was acting all goofy and (in his own weird way) flirty. He *had* to want to get back together.

And if he did . . . did she want that, too?

She honestly had no idea. Their time together seemed like a million years ago. It was like thinking about whether she wanted to go back to the fifth grade or something.

Jenna was so distracted, she barely noticed the time passing. But before she knew it, the bell was sounding to tell campers that lunch was over. It was time for afternoon activities—or, for today at least, *no* activities.

"So what are you going to do this afternoon?" Connor asked Nat.

"I'm not sure," she replied, sighing. "I guess I'll just hang close to my kids and see what *they* want to do. Actually, I had all these plans for activities for my campers because Dr. Steve said how important it was to keep them busy. But now I guess they're all scrapped. I kind of wish Brynn had asked us before she announced her big idea."

"I know," Sarah agreed looking like it pained her to criticize a friend. "I guess the afternoon sports sessions are canceled, so no volleyball for me. I guess I'll just write some letters—and then I can help you guys, Jenna and David."

Jenna shrugged. "You can help *me*," she said. "I'm sure David has stuff planned for the free period, right?" She looked at her ex, silently begging, *Please have something else planned. Please prove to me that you don't want to get back together.*

But David just looked at her, feigning shock. "Are you *kidding*?" he asked. "I'm in this to win this, baby. I'll meet you back at the secret location in five." He leaned over and squeezed her shoulder—Jenna felt herself stiffen, and hoped he didn't notice—then followed Priya, Ben, Nat, and Connor to the doors.

Jenna watched him, lost in thought. *I really don't need this right now.*

"Jenna?" Sarah asked in a timid voice, tapping her on the shoulder from behind.

"Yeah?" Jenna asked, embarrassed. She'd kind of

forgotten anyone else was still there.

"I have some letter-writing to catch up on, but I'll come help you with the balloons at three, okay?"

Jenna nodded, glancing at her watch. It was one now. And after all the headway they'd made this morning, she was feeling a little calmer about the afternoon. "Cool."

"And Jenna?"

Jenna looked up, and saw that Sarah looked hesitant, just a little awkward—like she wasn't sure whether she wanted to say something. "Yeah?" Jenna asked, hoping it wasn't anything big.

Sarah smiled. "I think it's really great that you and David are still so close, you know? You guys click so well." She waved quickly, and with that, disappeared through the doors.

Jenna shook her head, not sure what to think. She decided to throw herself into her work to take her mind off things—and practically ran back to the faculty bathroom.

chapter
EIGHT

"Sooooo . . . ," said Ben, slowing to a stop about thirty yards from the mess hall. He and Priya had been more or less wandering aimlessly, neither one of them wanting to say good-bye, but neither one brave enough to suggest another activity, either. At least, that was what Priya took away from it.

"So," she agreed, allowing herself a sincere smile. *This is really going so well,* she thought in amazement. She had to admit, when Nat had first suggested that she talk to Ben and see what they had in common, she'd had her doubts. Brynn had already made it clear that she and Ben were meant to be, and Priya almost felt like they couldn't *both* be right for Ben; if Brynn was, that meant Priya wasn't. And she didn't think she could force it.

And yet, when Nat had prodded the two of them to sit together at lunch, and forced them into conversation—it was amazing. Maybe their conversation hadn't happened naturally, but they were still getting to know each other. And while Ben wasn't *exactly* as she'd imagined him—he had a bigger personality, a louder laugh, and told more jokes—she still got butterflies in her stomach every time he smiled at her. She almost couldn't believe that *Ben*, this adorable guy she'd spent all last night crushing on, was actually standing in front of her, wanting to hang out.

Such was the magic of Nat.

Priya hesitated. She was dying to ask Ben to spend the afternoon with her. She thought maybe they could get some juice and granola bars from the mess hall, grab her camera, and take a private hike around the lake. Maybe—just maybe—things would even get more romantic between them, with nobody else around.

But each time she tried to get the words out, she stopped. It was weird—Priya felt like she could say anything to Jordan, her best friend since childhood, and *he* was a boy. But this whole letting-boys-know-you-like-them thing and risking rejection—this was a lot tougher.

"Um," she said finally, forcing the sound out of her mouth. "Maybe we could . . ."

But before she could even finish, she noticed that Ben wasn't even looking at her. He was staring over her shoulder at someone coming out of the mess hall. "Hey, Brynn!" he called.

Priya froze. *Oh, no. Not Brynn.* She knew that she and her friends were all in agreement about her having dibs on Ben, but *Ben* didn't know that. If Brynn was right . . . if they really had an amazing connection . . . what was to stop him from trying to hang out with her?

Brynn looked up, smiled, and came running over. "Hey," she said lightly, not even looking directly at him. She smiled down at Priya. "I see you met my friend Priya. Isn't she, like, the coolest chick ever?"

Priya felt a wave of relief wash over her even before Ben turned to face her. *Brynn's totally trying to help me. She would never make a play for him now.* And when Ben's eyes met hers, warm and interested, she felt even better. *He totally does like me.* "Sure," he agreed. "Did you know she takes awesome photos? She was just telling me."

Brynn nodded. "She's super-talented. Anyway . . ." She looked over at the camp offices, eager to excuse herself from the conversation.

"I just wanted to say," Ben continued, turning back to Brynn, "that was kick-butt what you did back in there. Everyone was getting all bent out of shape about lunch, and you totally won them back to your side. You *should* be Dr. Steve someday, Brynn. That was totally a leader move."

Brynn paused, her eyes suddenly warming. "Really?" she asked. "I haven't, like, been in charge much before. I mean I've directed some plays, but . . ."

"You direct?" Ben asked, sounding as impressed as if Brynn had just announced she'd invented a cancer vaccine.

Brynn shrugged. "Just at my school."

"Don't be modest," Ben teased, and Priya felt her throat constricting. *This is not good. Not good. Not . . .*

"Hey, so, what are you going to do this afternoon, Brynn?" Priya asked, desperate to change the subject.

"Important head of camp business? Do you have to, like, meet with other heads of camp? Maybe in another state?"

Brynn laughed. "*Priya*. Sheesh. Such an imagination." She smiled at Ben, and he winked at her. Priya felt like she was screaming inside. "No, I have a free afternoon just like everyone else. What are you guys doing?"

Not what you're doing. "We're, um, thinking of going . . ." Priya began.

But Ben cut her off. "We don't have any real plans," he told Brynn.

"*Well*," Brynn said, leaning in to both of them like she had a secret. "This is all totally in the planning stages, but I'm trying to get a camp bus to take people into town—you know, just to walk around, shop, get ice cream, maybe. I figured, what could be less camplike than leaving camp?"

Ben nodded, clearly loving the idea. "Awesome!" he cried.

"Do you guys want to come?" Brynn asked. "I just have to check back at the office if they can spare the bus, and then we'll make an announcement, and leave fifteen minutes later."

Priya brought her hand up to her mouth, nervously chewing at her fingernail. She didn't want to go into town, not really. She barely had any money with her, and besides, she'd rather take pictures. But more than anything, she wanted to be with Ben. And she sensed he was losing interest in her, fast. "Well . . ." she said quietly.

"We'll go," Ben announced, nodding at Brynn before Priya could give her opinion. "That sounds really fun, right, Priya?"

He turned to her, and again, it was like someone turning on a heat lamp. His gaze was so warm and concerned, Priya felt her knees weakening. *Okay, maybe he really does like me!*

"Sure," she said, pulling her hand away from her mouth. "Sounds great."

"Cool. See ya then." Brynn smiled and took off to check in at the camp office. It wasn't until after she left that Priya remembered *her* "Opposite Day" job. Actually, at lunch, she'd noticed a few of her younger campers were among the kids upset by the new seating rules—but by the time she noticed, the *actual* counselors had left their posts as "campers" to comfort the kids. She'd kind of noticed a couple of the real counselors giving her sharp looks, but by then, there had been nothing for her to do.

Maybe I should check in with them now, she thought.

"So," Ben said, dazzling her with a warm smile, "you were saying something a minute ago? Something about 'maybe we should . . .'"

Priya looked at him, confused. At first she thought maybe *he* was trying to tell her she should check in with the younger kids. But then she remembered—before Brynn came along, she'd been about to ask him if he wanted to go hiking.

"Oh," she said. "Yeah, no biggie—I was just wondering, do you like hiking?"

"*Do I?*" asked Ben, looking thrilled that she'd

asked. As they strolled back across the lawn to the mess hall, taking their time, Ben told her a crazy story about going hiking in New Jersey with his cousin and getting totally lost. As he spoke, Priya wondered if she should interrupt him—*excuse me, but I have to run and check on my campers*—but she couldn't bring herself to do it. She was having too much fun with him. When was the last time she'd liked a boy who actually liked her back?

Besides . . . surely the younger kids would be okay on their own. It was a free period, anyway. And it wasn't like there weren't counselors with them . . . they just weren't supposed to be "in charge" today.

After a few minutes, Brynn came running out of Dr. Steve's office and over to them, looking totally excited. "It's a go!" she said happily. "They're making an announcement now over the camp speakers, and the bus will leave in fifteen minutes from the amphitheater."

Ben grinned. "Let's go, then," he said cheerfully, and the pleased look he gave Brynn might have broken Priya's heart—*if he hadn't reached out right then and put his hand on her shoulder!* She jumped, and Ben looked at her and laughed. "Sorry. Didn't mean to startle you."

"It's okay," insisted Priya, smiling. "It's totally okay." Together, the three of them began making their way to the amphitheater.

The conversation bounced and leaped, never pausing for more than a couple seconds. Priya had to admit that, yeah, Ben and Brynn seemed to have a lot in common, but he was also careful to include and say nice things about Priya, too. Stuff like, "Priya says she has a crazy little brother, too," or, "I can't take pictures to save my life, either—unlike Priya, here. You love it so much, Priya, you must be amazing!"

Priya felt her face flush at that last one. She may have exaggerated her interest a little—but only because Ben was so into theater, and she wanted to seem artistic, too. Besides, she really did love taking pictures. And she was improving every day!

Soon they reached the spot where the buses were idling, and as they stood around waiting, lots more campers showed up, all chatting eagerly about what they planned to do "in town." Camp Walla Walla wasn't located in a bustling metropolis or anything, but the town had a nice main street with some cute shops and restaurants. Priya fingered the few bills she had in her pocket, hoping that she could convince Brynn and Ben to get an ice cream, and then linger in the shop.

"Yeah," she agreed, when Ben commented that a lot of campers had showed up. "I guess people really have cabin fever! Get it?"

Ben snorted, but Brynn barely reacted at all. At first Priya was hurt, but then she realized that Brynn was looking *behind* her at something.

"Isn't that the counselor from one of the little-kid bunks?" Brynn asked.

Priya felt her heart leap into her throat. *Oh no!* She turned around, and sure enough, Gabbie, the counselor for the Cedar tent, was walking up to her with a decidedly unfriendly expression.

"Hey, Gabbie," she said, trying to make her voice sound chill and casual. "What's up?"

Gabbie furrowed her brows. "Where have you been?" she asked, sounding not chill and casual at all. "I've been looking all over for you. It's like you disappeared after lunch."

"Oh," breathed Priya, not sure what to say. "Well . . . I . . ."

Suddenly Gabbie looked behind Priya at the buses and the gathered crowd. "Wait a minute," she said, turning to her delinquent "boss." "You're not seriously thinking of leaving camp, are you? We have sixty little kids to take care of. We *need* you."

Priya gulped, shooting an embarrassed glance at Brynn and Ben. Brynn was biting her lip sympathetically, but Ben was staring down at his hands, like he was trying to remove himself from the conversation. "I was just . . . I . . . no, of course not." Priya sighed, feeling defeated.

"Good," said Gabbie with a curt nod. "Because Frankie and Elyssa—you know, the girls in Birch— they got into an argument and it actually got physical for a minute there."

Priya gasped. "Really?" She'd spent a little time with Birch that morning—all of the kids seemed so sweet!

"Yeah," Gabbie confirmed. "They get tired and cranky after lunch—you'll see. Anyway, we thought it would be a good idea for them to have some quiet time to calm down. They'll be hanging out in the cabin for a couple hours, and it's your job to watch them."

Priya took a deep breath. She'd been so close to spending her afternoon with her crush and one of her best friends, eating ice cream and trading stories— now she was about to spend it cooped up in a cabin, watching two angry eight-year-olds. Life could not be more unfair.

And then she had an even *more* horrible realization. If she was cooped up inside—all because, she realized suddenly, she'd traded jobs with Jenna—that left Ben and Brynn to go on their fun, potentially romantic, journey *alone*.

Without *her*.

But *with* each other.

She felt her heart sink.

"Well," she said slowly, looking at her friends with an apologetic expression. "I guess a younger kids' counselor's work is never done. I'll, um . . . I guess I'll catch up with you later?"

"Totally," Ben said quickly, smiling another one of his amazing smiles at her. "I'll look for you at dinner, okay? We can finish our talk about hiking."

Priya nodded.

"And I'm sure I'll see you later," Brynn added. "We've got, like, a whole evening of fun activities planned. Remember—Opposite Day isn't even close to over!"

Right. Opposite Day, as in I get to do the opposite of what I'd really like to do, Priya thought bitterly. "Okay," she agreed, backing away to follow Gabbie back toward the cabins. "Later, then."

"Later," agreed Brynn. And as she looked at Priya

and waved, making a sad face, Priya felt a little better. She knew she could trust Brynn. She'd agreed to the whole having-dibs thing, and besides, it wasn't like a boy and girl couldn't hang out together in a totally friends-only way. Wasn't that how it was with Jordan? Priya tried to imagine going into town with Jordan. It would be fun, it would be silly—but most of all, it would be totally platonic.

Of course, Priya didn't have a crush on Jordan.

And as she saw Ben turn back to Brynn with a huge megawatt smile, a little flurry of doubt swelled up in her heart.

chapter NINE

"*Oh my gosh!*" Brynn cried as she and Ben exited a funky antique store and back out onto the hot street. "You *are not* the world's biggest fan of *The Soup*! *I* am! Oh, dude, I quote it *all* the time."

Ben just smiled. "It's so . . . *meaty*," he said, quoting one of the show's famous catchphrases. "Yeah, I love Joel McHale. In fact, I would love to host that show someday. Can you imagine?"

Brynn grinned. She could *totally* imagine it—because she often fantasized about having that very job herself. Of course, all the hosts in the history of *The Soup* had a strong background in comedy, so if she really wanted it, she would have to bulk up her skills. "I really want to start a comedy improv group at school," she admitted, giving Ben a sly glance. "Am I crazy? I mean, it could be totally humiliating."

Ben gawped at her. "Are you *kidding?*" he asked. "It's like you have a window into my brain. I started one at my school in January—and yeah, we've totally humiliated ourselves *many* times, but we've had some great shows, too. And it's always fun."

Brynn bit her lip. She'd been smiling so much during their conversation, she wondered if she looked ridiculous. But it was hard *not* to smile when Ben was around. He just so totally, totally *got* her—talking to him was like talking to a male version of herself, but better. *Cuter.*

"Well," she said, trying to put her face back in a normal expression, "if I'm seeing correctly through that window into your mind, I believe I'm seeing a hankering for ice cream? A hankering that maybe Scoops down the street would help you out with."

Ben looked at her, shaking his head. "You're amazing," he said. "Are you craving ice cream, too?"

Brynn nodded. "Yup. I'm going to get . . ." She paused, grinning at him, challenging him to choose the same flavor.

Ben put his hand to his temple, like he was consulting a place deep inside his brain. "Cookie dough!" he shouted, at the same time Brynn announced, "Cherry vanilla!"

"Aw," said Ben, shaking his head in mock disappointment. "Can't win 'em all, I guess. And besides—*cherry vanilla?* Who gets that?"

Brynn shrugged. "I do," she replied. By this time, they had reached Scoops, so she pulled open the door and walked in.

Once they were settled at a booth, Brynn and Ben couldn't help poring over the menu, looking at the array of sundaes and treats that were available. "I don't think they serve *this* at the mess hall," Ben observed dryly, pointing at a photo of an enormous banana split.

Brynn nodded. "That thing is huge. Definitely a special-occasion sundae."

Ben closed his menu and looked directly into Brynn's eyes. "Well, I think this is," he said quietly, a smile spreading over his face. "A special occasion, I mean."

Brynn's heart pounded. On the one hand, that was *exactly* what she wanted to hear from Ben—some evidence that he liked her, that their connection was as obvious to him as it was to her. But at the same time, it was the *last* thing she wanted to hear. Hadn't she promised Priya and all her friends that she would let Priya have first "dibs"? Whatever that meant?

She swallowed, sticking her nose deep into the menu. "What do you think about brownie sundaes?" she asked, desperate to change the topic.

Ben laughed. "I *love* brownie sundaes. But you probably know that already. Just take how you feel about brownie sundaes, and that's probably how I feel, too. I mean—we have a lot in common."

Stop him. Stop him. "I hate brownie sundaes," she blurted. *Uh-oh. That sounds ridiculous. Nobody hates brownie sundaes.*

Ben smirked. He obviously thought she was kidding. "You do, huh?" he asked. "Why do you hate brownie sundaes?"

Brynn thought fast. *Think of this as an improv exercise,* she told herself. *You need to learn to think on your feet.* "A brownie sundae killed my grandmother," she said quickly, before she could think it over.

Now Ben laughed.

"I'm *serious*," Brynn insisted, willing the corners of her mouth to stay down.

Ben looked skeptical, but he stopped laughing. He looked at Brynn out from under his eyelashes, as if to ask, *Are you playing me?* But instead he sat up in his chair and asked seriously, "How did a brownie sundae kill your grandmother?"

Yikes. This improv stuff was harder than Brynn thought. "Well, she was, um, she ate a brownie sundae one day at this ice cream stand, right, and then she went to take the bus to get home. But she got hot fudge sauce on her shoes, right, from the sundae, and it was that special hot fudge that turns solid after awhile? Like an ice cream bar?"

Ben nodded, humoring her. "I don't think that technically counts as hot fudge, but all right," he agreed.

"Well," Brynn continued, sitting up in her chair, getting into her story now. "The bus came, right, and she went to move out of the way, but she had this chocolate sauce on her shoes and it had *hardened to the street* and she couldn't move!"

Ben opened his mouth. "Omigosh!" he cried. Clearly he didn't believe her for a second, but he was playing along.

Brynn shrugged. "Yeah, so the bus hit her," she went on, picking her menu back up. "And she died. Now I can never eat brownie sundaes."

She managed to keep a straight face as she desperately avoided looking Ben in the eye. She grabbed the menu and started flipping through it again—even though she'd known what she was going to order since before they walked in the door. Even as she stared down at the glossy pages, though, she felt her lips turning up. After a few seconds, Ben reached out and pushed the menu down, trying to meet her eye. The minute Brynn looked up at him, she burst out laughing.

"Omigod I'm sorry . . ." she gasped through her giggles.

Ben just watched her, smiling as he seemed to try to hold in his own laughter. "That was pretty good," he admitted.

Brynn couldn't stop laughing. "I'm sorry . . . I just . . . your face . . ."

Ben sighed. "They don't carry magic shell at ice cream stands," he told her, shaking his head. "Magic shell—the chocolate sauce that hardens. You happen to be speaking to an expert."

Brynn took a deep breath, trying to get ahold of herself. "I prefer the cherry stuff myself. As you can see, I'm a total cherry girl."

Ben rolled his eyes. "Cherry is for amateurs." He paused, tilting his head as his gaze intensified. "That may be the one thing we disagree on."

Oh no. Abort! Abort! Brynn struggled to look away. Finally, she just looked down at her hands. "I guess."

Ben watched her for a moment, quiet, like he was trying to gather up his courage. After what seemed like hours, but was probably only a few seconds, he asked, "So . . . do you think you could stoop to hang out with a guy who likes brownie sundaes and prefers chocolate magic shell to cherry?"

Brynn's heart pounded in her chest. She opened her mouth to reply, but couldn't get the words out. *What do I do? What do I do?* "Well . . . ," she said finally, "I'm kind of busy today."

Ben laughed, like he knew she was kidding again. "Sure," he responded. "I can see you're really up to your ears in important camp business."

Brynn swallowed. *Must say no, must act uninterested.* "Have you, um . . . haven't you been spending a lot of time with Priya?" she asked, hopefully.

Ben looked surprised. "Priya?" he asked. "I just met her at lunch."

Brynn nodded. "But she's cool, right?" she asked, not sure how she wanted him to answer. "*Really* cool."

Ben made a funny face. "Sure," he replied. "She's a lot of fun to talk to. Really enthusiastic and stuff. I'm glad I met her. She'll be a good friend."

Friend. Brynn let the word echo in her ears, over and over. "So . . . you don't want to go out with Priya?" she asked, not sure whether to feel relieved or disappointed. After all, where did this leave her?

"Go out with Priya?" Ben chuckled, shaking his head. "I never even thought about it. She's great, I mean. I just . . ." He met Brynn's eyes, his expression warm. "I guess I already kind of had a crush on someone when I met her."

Brynn's heart was pounding a mile a minute now. She swallowed, trying to think of something to say. But in the end, she came up with nothing. She had no idea what to do. She just knew she had to keep Ben from thinking she liked him back—at least until she had a chance to think.

Instead of meeting his eye, Brynn raised her hand, signaling the waitress who was picking up her tip a few tables away. "Excuse me, miss?" she called. "I think we're ready to order. And I *really* need some ice cream."

▲ ▲ ▲

"Just . . . fill . . . them . . . *up!*" Brynn heard Jenna shrieking as she entered the overcrowded faculty bathroom in the mess hall. Sarah, David, Jenna, and what had to be hundreds of filled-up water balloons filled every inch of the already-tiny space.

David, who had uninflated balloons hanging from each finger, sighed patiently. "I was just showing you guys my tadpole impression," he said, making some halfhearted swimming motions with his arms.

Jenna widened her eyes even more, which made her look a lot like an extra in a zombie movie. "Are you kidding me, David?" she practically shouted. "We don't have *time* for this! We have to make the Prank to End All Pranks happen in *two hours!* Do you get that? Do we look anywhere near done here?"

Brynn looked down at the boxes of balloons by Jenna's feet. "How many are we filling up?" she asked, timidly.

"All of them," Sarah replied, shooting Brynn a sympathetic look. Brynn wondered how long Sarah had been cooped up in this room with the bickering exes. David seemed used to Jenna stressing out about her pranks, but he also seemed to know exactly how to push her buttons.

Jenna turned to Brynn, taking notice of her for the first time, and nodded. She grabbed the box from the floor and held it up, showing her the contents. "That's right, all of them," she told Brynn, shaking the box as what had to be hundreds of balloons bounced inside. "And we've got two more boxes left after that. Can you see why I'm stressed out?"

Brynn took a deep breath. "It'll be okay, Jenna," she cooed trying to sound soothing and calm, like the woman on the relaxation CDs her mom listened to sometimes. "What do you need me to do? It'll go faster now that there are four of us."

Jenna sighed, looking around at the masses of filled balloons that threatened to spill out of the bathroom at any second. "Tie up the balloons," she replied brusquely. "David will show you how to do it. I'm going to get some garbage bags and try to get as many of these out of here as I can."

"Okay," Brynn agreed, and then waited for Jenna to squeeze herself out of the space she stood in so she could take her place. Moving next to David, who by now had removed all the balloons from his fingers and was getting back to work, she held out her hands.

"All right," she told David. "Lay it on me."

After a quick instruction course from David, Brynn got pretty good at tying off the balloons and placing them in a pile—so good, in fact, that she no longer had to think about it. David and Sarah still seemed to be in pretty good moods, and at first, Brynn traded quips with them, happily engaging in their conversation. But as time went on . . . and the balloon-filling-up took on more of a rhythm . . . her mind started to wander.

Back to Ben.

He was *so* cute. With his light brown hair and his funny vintage T-shirts. And the way he told a story, using his hands and throwing his whole body into it, looking up at her every once in a while as if to say, *You know? Are you still with me? Isn't this crazy?*

The way he loved all the same things she loved, and the way he totally understood when she talked about acting and theater and her dreams—because they were his dreams, too. Brynn was reminded of the way things were when she and Jordan first got together.

And he liked her. That much was obvious now. The way he'd looked at her, the way he even got nervous (aww!) before asking her to hang out with him again. That was *super*sweet.

But before Brynn could let herself get carried away thinking about Ben and the awesome future the two of them could have together, her mind kept coming back to one thing.

Priya.

Priya had "dibs" on Ben.

But then . . . what did that mean, really? That morning, Brynn had agreed to give Priya a shot with Ben. To let her get to know him, see if they had anything in common. Hadn't she done that? When Nat put them together at lunch, and when they were talking on the lawn later, she hadn't done anything to interfere. In fact, she'd tried to show Ben how great Priya was.

But now, hours later, Ben had told her that he saw Priya as a friend. That wasn't Brynn's fault. It was just the way it was.

So did it make sense for *neither* of them to get the guy they wanted?

No, Brynn realized, violently tying up the end of a balloon David handed her. *No, it did not.*

But now what? She'd spent the whole remainder of their time in town trying to avoid eye contact or any conversation deeper than "that's a cool bike" with Ben. She knew he liked her, but she seriously doubted he had any inkling just how much she liked him. And now that she realized she was totally within her rights to be straight with him . . . well, she couldn't wait. Maybe if she arranged an event where they could spend a little more time together. Maybe fate would just take over, and she could hang out with Ben, guilt-free.

Brynn took a deep breath. Then it came to her: the event that night! Jenna had asked Tricia to plan something they could all be heading to when the balloon fight broke out. But maybe, just maybe, the balloon fight could be *after* the event. And maybe the event could be something . . . romantic. Or at least, with the possibility for romance. A dance? No, they couldn't have a dance at night—today was Opposite Day.

Then it came to her. The perfect idea.

And if she planned it so only the older kids could go . . .

Brynn dropped the balloon she'd been holding. Thankfully, it just bounced lazily on the edge of the sink and then fell in. Jenna moved behind her—she'd been coming in and out the whole time, bagging up water balloons and moving them out of the bathroom. By now, she'd actually cleared enough space that the four of them could all stand there comfortably.

Instead of picking up her balloon, Brynn whirled around to her friend. "Jenna," she announced, "I gotta go. I'm sorry. Important camp business. It just came up . . ." Wiping her wet hands on her shorts, Brynn angled around Jenna and started striding toward the door. She had to find Tricia!

chapter
TEN

"Are you *kidding* me?" Jenna grabbed Brynn's arm and spun her around before she could disappear out the faculty bathroom door. "What? You're leaving? What about tip-teep? What about making Camp Walla Walla history? You realize we have, like, ninety minutes tops to get all these balloons filled, don't you?"

Brynn turned to face Jenna, but she had a faraway look in her eyes. Jenna could tell she was barely listening. "What? Oh, don't worry, Jenna. I'll be back to help—I mean, if I can."

Jenna raised an eyebrow. "*If you can?* What are you doing, anyway? What's so important that it has to be done right now?"

Brynn made an impatient move toward the door. "It's . . . it's . . . nothing. Just some night swimming after dinner tonight *before* the water-balloon fight. That will be fun, right? Everyone loves to swim, and it's more fun at night!"

Jenna couldn't believe what she was hearing. She shook her head, unable to comprehend her friend's words. "What do you mean before the water-balloon fight?" she asked. "We all agreed it would happen right after dinner. When everyone is headed out to Tricia's event."

Brynn shrugged. Jenna could tell these details weren't nearly as important to Brynn as they were to her. "So we'll just do it *after* instead," Brynn suggested. "When everyone's headed back to their tent. It'll be perfect, actually—they'll all be dried off from swimming, and nobody will be expecting it." She paused, then smiled nervously at Jenna. "In fact, isn't that better?" she asked. "It will give you more time to prepare. And you can, like, calm down."

Jenna pulled her mouth into a taut line, thinking this over. It was true—they needed more time to fill the balloons. And yeah, hitting everyone when they were tired and on their way back to their tents to sleep was . . . kind of awesome, actually. Nobody would expect it.

Still. She didn't like Brynn switching things around like this, without even consulting her. "Why do you want the night swimming?" she asked. "This doesn't have anything to do with seeing that Ben kid in his bathing suit, does it?" She was *so* not going to see T.P.T.E.A.P. thwarted because of some stupid boy.

Brynn's cheeks turned pink, but otherwise she barely reacted to Jenna's question. "I just wanted to plan a fun activity," she insisted. "Besides, as Dr. Steve for the day, I'd like to add something fun to the schedule. Something for everyone to remember me by." She smiled.

Jenna breathed in. "Okay," she agreed. "But if you

can come back—please do."

"Of course," Brynn replied with a smile, but she was out the door before Jenna could utter another syllable.

Jenna sighed, turning from the now-closed door back to Sarah and David, who looked completely exhausted. Brynn *had* helped speed balloon production along, but they still had almost a full box left.

"All right," Jenna barked. "Let's get going! We still have balloons to fill!"

But Sarah and David just looked at each other out of the corner of their eyes, and neither of them moved. Jenna felt her frustration building. "I *said*—"

"We heard you," David said quickly, in a gentle voice. "But Jenna, seriously. You're pretty stressed out. And we just got, like, a two-hour extension—could we at least take a fifteen-minute break?"

"Yeah," Sarah agreed, looking a little frightened of Jenna. "You look like you could use it."

Jenna took a deep breath. Stopping even for a few minutes made her nervous, but she couldn't argue with their math; even taking fifteen minutes to rest, they were still an hour and forty-five minutes ahead of where they were before Brynn made her announcement. "Okay," she said, shaking her head to show that even if she agreed, it still pained her a little.

David grinned. "Cool, Jenna." Stepping toward her, he squeezed her shoulder. "I knew you'd come around."

Jenna stepped aside to let David and Sarah through, trying not to think about that shoulder squeeze. All afternoon, actually, she'd noticed that David was still in DAVID! mode. Making lots of jokes, being loud, telling crazy stories that Jenna knew for herself were pretty exaggerated. But still, she caught him *looking* at her all the time. Waiting for her reaction. No matter how many times she didn't laugh, or didn't act interested.

It was like he was trying to win her over.

Now she followed David and Sarah down the hall, out the doors of the mess hall, and into the too-bright sunshine. Used to the fluorescent lights of the bathroom, she squinted and shaded her eyes. David and Sarah walked about halfway across the lawn, and Jenna trailed them. Finally, David and Sarah sat down in a shaded area that overlooked the lake. Jenna plopped down a few feet away.

"So," David said.

"So," Sarah echoed.

"So," Jenna agreed. They were all exhausted. Jenna, especially, felt way too tired to keep a conversation going.

"I think we should throw out topics for conversation," David suggested. "Stuff that will expand our minds, you know, and make us smarter people. Topic one: Britney's *Circus* is a superior album to *Oops!. . . I Did It Again.* Discuss."

Jenna couldn't help laughing a little, and Sarah snorted. ". . . *Baby One More Time* beats either of those," Sarah insisted. "It's classic. Old-school."

David nodded sagely. "Well-argued," he allowed. "What about you, Jenna? What is your position?"

Jenna was looking out at the lake, picturing that box of unfilled balloons. "My position is that we need to get those balloons filled up."

Sarah groaned. "Oh, come on, Jenna. You must have some opinions on Britney Spears."

Jenna sighed. "I think she peaked with 'Toxic,'" she said finally. "That song is *catchy*. David, what's another topic?"

David looked at his hand, pretending to consult a list. "Next topic," he said, "is Ben & Jerry's. Resolved: New York Super Fudge Chunk is the best flavor."

Sarah shook her head. "Oh, come on," she insisted. "As a Red Sox fan, I don't think I can get behind anything that has 'New York' in the title."

Jenna couldn't help smiling. "Everyone knows that Phish Food is *far* superior," she said. "I mean, those little fish? What other ice cream flavor has little animals made out of chocolate in it?"

David looked thoughtful. "That gives me an idea. Platypus Crunch. It has vanilla ice cream, blackberries, a butterscotch ribbon, and little white chocolate platypuses scattered throughout."

Sarah frowned. "Why blackberries?" she asked.

David turned to her, looking at her like she was crazy. "For *color*," he replied. "*Hello.*"

Jenna grinned. "If you were going to make a Camp Walla Walla flavor, what would you put in it?"

Sarah and David both looked thoughtful.

"PB&J," David began. "For sure."

Sarah nodded. "And you would need some toasted marshmallows," she added. "Maybe even a whole s'more?"

"High drama," David added, nodding sagely. "There would have to be a lot of drama, especially from the girl bunks."

Jenna rolled her eyes. "And there would have to be high *stupidity* content," she added. "For the boys."

Sarah looked thoughtful. "Is there a way to put water balloons in an ice cream?"

Jenna laughed. David chuckled, too. "If there's a way," he said, "Jenna here will find it. Nobody loves water balloons like Miss Jenna, trust me." With that, he leaned over and squeezed Jenna's shoulder—*again*.

And suddenly the spell was broken, and Jenna felt super-stressed out again.

She jerked her shoulder away and stood up.

"Hey," Sarah said, shielding her eyes as she looked up at Jenna with a confused expression. "Where are you—"

But Jenna was already moving. She stalked away, across the lawn, past the mess hall, over toward the woods that faced the lake. The campgrounds were quiet; here and there, small groups of campers talked or played, but with everyone free to do their own thing, there were no organized activities. And it being almost dinnertime, the lake was nearly empty. Jenna sat on a boulder and looked out at the water. She struggled to take deep, calming breaths: *Calm down. It's all right. It's fine.* She felt her heartbeat slowing, and she closed her eyes.

Why now? she wondered, letting out a sigh. *Why is he doing this now?*

Within a few minutes, she heard footsteps behind

her. They didn't surprise her at all; she knew David would follow her. She knew she would have to talk to him about why she freaked. But more than anything, she wanted to put this conversation off until tomorrow, when she'd be less stressed and would have had more time to think. But it looked like that was going to be impossible.

Besides, she kind of knew what she had to say.

"Hey," David said gently, almost apologetically, like he used to when they were going out and he knew he'd made her mad. "So, uh, that was weird."

Jenna didn't say anything. She looked down at her hands, wishing she were anywhere else.

"Are you mad at me?" David asked. "Did I do something? Because if so, I'm really sorry."

Jenna gulped and turned around. David was standing right behind her, looking at her with concerned eyes.

"No," she said. "You didn't do anything. It's just . . ." She trailed off.

"It's just?" David prodded her.

Jenna took a deep breath. "I really care about you, David, and I always will. I hope you know that. You're one of my favorite people. I hope I'll always be your friend." She paused.

David stared at her, looking lost. "Okay. And . . .?"

Jenna swallowed again. "And I don't want to get back together," she whispered. "I'm sorry. When we were together, it was great, but it's just . . . it's so much *simpler* now. And right now, I really like simple. I think you're great. I just . . ." She paused, looking down at the ground. "I just can't."

David was silent for awhile. Maybe it was only seconds, but it felt like forever to Jenna. When she finally looked up at him, needing to see his reaction, she was surprised to see that he wasn't even looking at her. He was staring off into the distance, looking perplexed, like he was trying to figure out a puzzle and he didn't have all the pieces.

After a few seconds, he noticed Jenna staring and turned back to her. "What makes you think I want to get back together?" he asked.

Jenna shrugged. *Because I know you*, she thought, but she didn't say it aloud. "Because you're around all the time—eating lunch with us, hanging out. And lately it's like you've been SUPER David. You're all hammy, telling jokes and stories, like you're trying to impress me. And you're touchy all of a sudden. Plus, all my friends think you're acting this way because . . . you like me again."

David nodded. "Did you ever think . . ." he started, then paused. "Did you ever think that maybe I was hanging around because I was trying to be near someone else?"

Jenna just looked at him. She couldn't quite process what he was saying. "What?"

He moved in again, placing his hand gently on her shoulder, like before. This time, she didn't pull away. "Jenna," he said, his throat dry. "Would it really bother you if I hung out with Sarah at the night swim?"

chapter
ELEVEN

To: chacelvr@fastmail.net
From: priyadayada@internet.com
Re: What's the opposite of opposite?

OK Jules,

I am having kind of a not-great day.

I mean, it started out okay. Like I told you, we won the talent show last night, which meant we got to run the camp today. But it ended up that we had to choose positions out of a hat, and I gave away my low-key position as counselor to the older kids to help out my friend. So now I'm counselor to the younger kids. Have you ever been around younger kids, like REALLY been around them? I'm talking about eight- and nine-year-olds here. It turns out, they are REALLY loud and energetic, and they don't exactly like to do what you tell them to . . . especially if they're already mad because they're being punished for trying to shove each other (long story).

Anyway, I FINALLY got a chance to talk to

that Ben guy, the new love of my life, and he's awesome! Really sweet and smart, and I think he likes me back. But then, just when I was going to leave to spend the afternoon with him in town, I got called back here to stay with the kids during rest hour. It was anything but restful, though. These kids have SO much energy. Finally I found a copy of *Island of the Blue Dolphins* that somebody must have left behind one year and read to them until they calmed down.

In a few minutes, it's time for dinner, and then (I hope!) we'll all have some big camp activity tonight, so I'll get to see Ben (and my friends) again. I hate to say it, but I kind of can't wait to be done with Opposite Day. It turns out running the camp is not as fun as you would think . . .

—Priya

"Oh. . . my . . . gosh," Priya drawled, sidling up to the table in the dining hall where Jenna was sitting alone, staring into space. "I am so happy to see you."

Jenna looked up at Priya, her expression suspicious. "Yeah," she agreed. "How come you never came to help fill balloons?"

Priya sighed. "Because I've been locked up in a cabin with two delinquent eight-year-olds since lunch, practically." She looked around. "Where is everyone?"

Jenna shrugged. "Probably just running late from their amazing, relaxing afternoons doing whatever they wanted," she said with a sigh, then looked down at the table. "And . . . I don't know if David's going to sit with us tonight."

Priya was about to ask why when suddenly Nat bounced up to the table, followed closely by Connor and—*Ben!* Priya had to bite her lip to keep from totally beaming. She looked at Ben with what she hoped was a sly smile. "What's up?" she asked, trying to sound casual.

"Not much," said Ben, a casual smile forming on his lips. "How are your campers? How did it go?"

Priya shrugged. She didn't feel like going into the whole ordeal with Ben—she'd vent to her friends later. "It was okay," she said, "but I'm looking forward to getting to hang with the older kids tonight, let's just put it that way."

He smiled. Sarah came over and sat down then, shooting Jenna a small smile and looking around at the table. "Hey, guys," she said cheerily. "Everyone have a good afternoon?"

As Priya sat down at the table, the conversation wandered to what everyone had done that afternoon, how T.P.T.E.A.P. was going, and when Chelsea came running over a few minutes later, what they were having for Opposite Day dinner. It all felt great and comfortable and easy after Priya's tiring afternoon, and she finally felt like this was the camp she knew— the camp before Opposite Day. The thrill of talking to Ben and having him really listen to her was still as strong as it had felt at lunch. Could this really be the right guy for her? Could it really be this easy?

But just before Sarah left to pick up food for the

table, Ben pointed toward the front of the mess hall and asked, "What's Brynn up to?" Priya looked where he was pointing, and sure enough, Brynn was walking up to the microphone, like she was getting ready to make another announcement.

"Maybe she's going to announce that Opposite Day is over," suggested Priya hopefully. "You know, thanks for playing, back to your regularly scheduled programs . . ."

"I sure *hope* not," huffed Jenna, sitting up straight and alert.

Oops. Priya had nearly forgotten about the water-balloon fight. Well, that would be fun, she guessed. Anything that involved freedom would be fun.

Brynn grabbed the mike off its stand and smiled at all the assembled campers. "Good evening, campers," she said. "I hope you guys have all been having an awesome Opposite Day!"

A few of the younger kids applauded, but mostly, Brynn's statement was met by grumbles and skeptical looks. Priya was surprised. She knew at lunch the campers had had some issues with the way it was going so far, but hadn't the free afternoon erased those concerns? Hadn't everybody had a really good time?

"I'm bored," one of the older boys, a seventh-grader, called from the back of the hall. "When do we start activities again?"

"Yeah," agreed another boy sitting at the same table. "I'm sick of these pajamas! When do I get to take them off?"

"*Not* now," replied Brynn quickly, with a clever

smile, and a few laughs echoed through the mess hall. "But I hear you guys. I think you'll be really excited to hear my plans for the night, though."

Everyone seemed to sit up in their seats a little, eager to hear what Brynn had planned.

"First of all," Brynn went on, "divisions three, four, five, and six will go on a special night hike led by Dr. Steve." She smiled over at Dr. Steve where he was sitting in camper mode at one of the middle school tables, and he waved, clearly excited about the hike. "There will be no flashlights," Brynn went on. "Only the light of the moon. This will be a great chance for you guys to experience the special beauty of the woods at night."

A few of the kids *ooh*ed and *ahh*ed. Most seemed like they weren't sure about this latest development. Priya was feeling a little unsure herself. So if the younger and middle-aged kids got their own activity . . . did that mean . . .

"Meanwhile," Brynn went on, "there will be a special night swimming party for divisions seven and eight! After dinner, you'll have an hour to make your way back to your tents and get your bathing suits on, and then I'll meet you at the lake! Drinks and snacks will be provided!"

Several of the older kids cheered. But equally loud were some of the younger and middle-aged campers groaning or booing or yelling, "It's not fair!" Priya wasn't feeling like this was terribly fair herself. If only the older campers could go . . . technically, she *was* an older camper, but this was Opposite Day, and so . . .

"You'll have to stay with the kids you're watching, right, Priya?" asked Nat, looking disappointed. "That stinks. We won't get to hang out with you at the party."

Priya gulped. Nat was right; no getting around it. "I guess so," she agreed with a sigh.

"Maybe you'll be able to come for part of it," Sarah suggested. "Like, if the kids fall asleep . . ."

Priya sighed. "I doubt it," she admitted. "I learned that lesson this afternoon. We're supposed to stay with them and watch them . . . no matter how okay they might seem."

It might have been wishful thinking on Priya's part, but she thought she saw a disappointed expression pass over Ben's face. "Well, you're a very responsible counselor, Priya," he said after a moment, looking over at Brynn.

And then she saw it. Brynn smiled again, placed the microphone back onto the stand, and started walking back to her table. But right before she left the front of the room, she looked over at their table, met Ben's eye, and winked.

Priya felt her face growing hot.

Brynn. With her Dr. Steve position and her crush on Ben. There was no question, now, what had inspired this little "party." It couldn't be a coincidence that Brynn spent the whole afternoon alone with Ben . . . only to come back and plan a surprise "party" that Priya coincidentally wouldn't be able to attend.

But I have dibs! Priya thought furiously. *We all agreed!*

"Well, I'm sure you're not missing much," Jenna announced as Sarah went up to get their food. "Who wants to swim at night, anyway?"

Nat glanced at Jenna, looking a little surprised. "But then . . . tip-teep is still on for tonight, right?"

Jenna nodded. "Right after," she confirmed. "I mean, if nothing happens to screw it up."

Priya sighed. She was having trouble trying to act like she wasn't disappointed. She knew the whole idea of Opposite Day was for the campers to experience what it was really like for the counselors, but she got it already . . . it was tough. She didn't ever want to be a camp counselor for third- and fourth-graders. Duly noted. Could she go to the party now?

"Well," Nat said gently, seeming to notice Priya's upset expression. "At least we only have a few more hours of Opposite Life. Then we go to bed, and when we wake up, it'll just be a normal day at camp."

Priya sighed. "Tomorrow morning can't come quickly enough."

▲ ▲ ▲

A couple hours later, Priya was laying on the counselor's bunk bed in one of the younger kids cabins, listening to the sound of her own heartbeat. It was superquiet outside—except every couple minutes or so, Priya would hear laughing or splashing from the night swim party. The lake was a good hundred yards away, if not more, but the noise traveled far because it was so quiet. *And probably just to torture me,* Priya added to herself. Really, after the day she'd had, it was hard to believe someone out there wasn't reveling in her pain.

The night hike with Dr. Steve had gone okay, though some of the campers grumbled the whole time about not getting to go night swimming. All the third- and fourth-level campers had gone to bed about half an hour before, and now it sounded like they'd finally all fallen asleep. For the first few minutes, Priya had had to keep going in there, breaking up whispered conversations and fights. *Were we ever like that when we first came to camp?* Priya wondered. It was hard to imagine. She and her friends had been going to camp for so long, it almost felt like they'd *always* been experts, never newbies.

But today, Priya felt like a newbie in at least one way: She had no idea how to compete for a boy. She felt like she had a stomachache every time she thought of Brynn's little wink to Ben in the mess hall. Really, what part of *dibs* did she not understand? And throwing this whole silly party tonight while Priya was stuck in this stupid bunk? *So* not cool. Priya thought she and her bunkmates were all friends, that they had each other's backs. But clearly Brynn was only out for herself.

Priya sighed. She felt like, of all the girls at camp, she was *never* out for herself. Not before her friends, anyway. In fact . . . sometimes it seemed like she was always putting her friends' happiness above her own. Like when she'd gone along with Brynn's talent show skit idea, even though she thought hers was funnier.

Or how she'd given up her easy "older kids' counselor" job for Jenna . . . even though she *hadn't* wanted to work with the younger kids at all. All so Jenna could work on her dumb prank.

Staring up at the ceiling, she took a deep breath. A loud laugh echoed off of the lake, followed by a loud *sploosh* of someone getting pushed into the water. *I always do this,* Priya thought. *I always do the nice thing, the "right" thing. Even if it's not right for me.*

She bit her lip, Sarah's words at dinner suddenly echoing in her ear. *Maybe you'll be able to come for part of it* . . . When she'd said it, Priya had immediately said no, she had to stay with her kids. But now, it had been at *least* half an hour since she'd heard anything besides even breathing from the kids. And, besides, it's not like she'd be leaving them *totally* alone . . . there was a counselor (a real one) on night watch already. If anything came up with these campers . . . surely she could take care of it.

Priya sat up slowly. She looked around, then swung her feet off the bed, half-waiting for someone to spring into the room and yell at her: *"What are you doing? You can't do that!"* But no one came. Priya was alone. And if she wanted to go to the party, just for a few minutes—if that's what she *really* wanted—nobody was going to stop her.

". . . totally lame," Priya heard a seventh-grader named Todd scoff. She was on her way to the lake when she passed by a table that was totally decimated. A couple empty bags of chips and three empty bottles of soda littered the ground nearby. "I can't believe they thought this was enough food."

As she got closer to the beach, she heard some tinny music playing on someone's iPod that had been plugged into a couple of tiny speakers. To make up for the speakers' size, whoever had set it up had turned the volume up to ten. As a result, the song was so distorted and there was so much feedback, it was hard to tell who was actually singing.

But as soon as she reached the lake, all of her concerns about the party disappeared. Because there, right in front of her, were Brynn and Ben. They sat together on a raft in the middle of the lake, chatting and laughing. As Priya watched, Ben suddenly reached out and pushed a lock of Brynn's hair behind her ear. Brynn beamed at him. It was like something out of a cheesy romantic comedy.

Gross, thought Priya.

Since she'd been busy watching the younger kids, she hadn't had time to get her bathing suit. She'd stormed down to the lake in Nat's pajamas, which she'd been wearing all day. But clearly, one, Brynn had to be stopped, and two, this was not the kind of situation that could wait for a costume change. She kicked off Nat's flip-flops, arranging them neatly on the beach, away from the water. Then she waded right in—pj's and all.

It took her a few minutes to get out to the raft, but thankfully, Priya was such a quiet swimmer, or else Brynn and Ben were so involved in their conversation, they didn't hear her approach. It wasn't until Priya grabbed onto a rope hanging from the side of the raft and began clambering up that they took notice of her at all.

"*Priya?*" Brynn asked, squinting at the girl before her, whose wet, dripping pajamas clung to her like a pile of wet rags. "Are you . . . what are you doing?"

Priya smiled coldly. "I'm just taking a dip on a hot night, Brynn," she replied. "What are *you* doing?"

chapter

TWELVE

Brynn couldn't believe her eyes. Had Priya just risen out of the lake like the Loch Ness Monster—*in her pajamas?* And wasn't she supposed to be watching her campers? After all, Brynn had purposely planned this party as an *older campers only* thing. Not to exclude Priya, exactly—younger kids just weren't strong enough swimmers yet to be trusted in the dark—but, um, yeah, getting Priya out of the picture had been an added bonus.

And so far, her plan had been *working*, big-time. She and Ben had barely spent a second apart since the party started a couple hours ago. They'd discussed their shared love of grape soda ("the forgotten soda") by the refreshment stand; got into a pretty serious splashing fight in the shallow water; had an underwater race to the raft (Brynn won); and, for the last twenty minutes or so, had just sat in the moonlight, talking and laughing. She couldn't help it: She was *way* into Ben, and it was pretty clear that he was way into her, too. Some of her bunkmates at the party had been shooting her dirty looks, but she couldn't be bothered by that. She and

Ben were just meant to be. And she'd planned to come clean to them all later that night—even Priya.

But it looked like Priya wasn't willing to wait.

"Um," Brynn said now, glancing from Ben to her waterlogged friend and back. "Ben and I were just talking about *The Dark Knight*. Have you seen it?"

It was true—specifically, they'd been talking about how Heath Ledger had done such an amazing job as the Joker, and how they'd read that he really threw himself into the role.

Priya's eyes lit up. "That's the one with Christian Bale?" she asked. "Oh, man, I *love* Christian Bale. I think he's really cute."

As she spoke, Priya casually-but-not-really scooted over to Ben and plopped down on his other side, dripping water all over the raft. "Did you like *The Dark Knight*, Ben?" she asked, smiling up at him.

Ben glanced awkwardly back at Brynn. "Um, yeah," he admitted. "I thought it was cool, actually. It was about Batman, but you didn't have to love him to love the movie. You know?"

Brynn nodded energetically, hoping to wrest the conversation back from Priya. "Totally," she agreed. "I think a lot of that was because the actors were so good."

"Yeah," Ben agreed. "Heath Ledger and Christian Bale are both such great actors. That's all that really matters, ya know? That's why I never get it when people complain about actors not being, like, totally nice when they ask for an autograph. That's not their *job*, you know?"

Priya looked confused. "Wait . . . you don't feel bad for the people they're not nice to?" she asked. "But it doesn't take a lot of energy to just be polite. I think people should be nice to people who are being nice to them. Even if he is a *star* and the other person is just a lowly fan or whatever."

Priya's comment was met by silence. Secretly, Brynn agreed with Priya, but she wasn't going to say that out loud in front of Ben.

After a few moments of nobody saying anything, Brynn took the opportunity to ask: "Priya, who's watching your campers? Aren't you supposed to be in the tent?"

Priya looked stung, and she quickly turned away, staring out across the lake, and shrugged. "I made a deal with one of my friends from another bunk," she muttered. "I just wanted to come to the party for a few minutes. Is that okay with *you?*"

Brynn, who wasn't exactly convinced that Priya was telling the truth, opened her mouth to reply, but she couldn't get any words out. For a few seconds, again, nobody said anything. Then suddenly, Ben spoke up.

"You know what?" he said, not looking directly at either girl. "I'm, um . . . I'm gonna swim back to the beach. It's just, um, it's getting kind of chilly out here, and I want my towel."

Priya sprung up immediately. "I'll go, too!" she said. "The music sounds great, huh? It kind of makes me want to dance."

Brynn drew her feet out of the water and stood

up, too. "Me too," she said quickly, before Ben could respond to Priya. "I should probably check on the refreshments and stuff."

Priya turned to Brynn with a satisfied glare. "The refreshments have been gone for awhile," she said. "People are complaining. Maybe you should go to the mess hall to get more."

Brynn looked at her friend, startled. "Well," she said after a few seconds, recovering, "it's kind of a last-minute party. I don't know what people expected—Jamie Oliver from The Food Network? I did the best I could on short notice."

Sploosh! Without warning, Ben leaped into the water and started paddling back to shore. "See you back there!" he called out to Priya and Brynn. But he didn't pause in his swimming, or look behind him.

Brynn shot Priya a look like, *Look what you've done!* Brynn felt her heart speeding up. Just a few minutes before, she'd been locked in an awesome conversation with the most perfect-for-her boy in the universe. Now, she felt like she was acting out a scene from a soap opera. And not one of the *good* scenes.

She glared at Priya. "I'm sorry, Priya, but Ben is *perfect* for me," she said in a low voice, once Ben was out of earshot. "I didn't mean to start liking him, but we really clicked. Can't you just let him go?"

Priya looked at Brynn like she was speaking Chinese. "But I have *dibs*," she insisted, shaking her head like this was the most obvious thing in the world. "And he likes me! We were having an awesome time together before *you* showed up this afternoon!

What part of *dibs* don't you understand?"

The whole thing, Brynn wanted to spit back, *because dibs are stupid when it comes to boys!* But she didn't say that. And she didn't think she could explain right then that Ben *didn't* like Priya that way, he was just being nice. So instead she jumped into the water and started swimming back. The lake felt warm and silky in the August night, and there was barely any wind. It was really the perfect night for swimming.

Sploosh! A few seconds after Brynn dived in, Priya followed. Brynn sighed, even as she paddled back to shore. Of *course* Priya wasn't going to give up. She was like that paper boy in that old '80s movie, *Better Off Dead*. "I want my two dollars!" Brynn could picture Priya haunting her and Ben for the rest of the summer, hanging around their romantic moments, clinging to the back of their bicycle-made-for-two. *"But I have dibs!"*

One thing was for sure. Brynn was never giving up "dibs" on a boy, ever again.

Once on shore, she stumbled to her feet and started walking. She meant to follow Ben, who had run over to a picnic table where he'd left his towel and was drying off, facing away from her. But before she could get very far, a well-manicured hand reached out of nowhere and grabbed Brynn's arm.

"Hey," a sharp voice said. "We have to talk."

Brynn turned around and let out a sigh.

Nat.

"Okay, *obviously* Priya is upset," Nat said, leaning against a tree in the little glade where they'd gone to have their "talk." "She just jumped into the lake in my Calvin Klein pajamas. I mean, I understand, but . . ."

Brynn just shook her head. "I forgot those were yours."

Nat sighed. "This isn't like you," she insisted. "Stealing someone else's guy. You're not usually a selfish person. But ever since this party started, you've been all over Ben like white on rice."

Brynn groaned inwardly. Nat made her sound pathetic and desperate, but Brynn knew the truth. "I've been hanging around Ben because he wants to hang around *me*," Brynn insisted. "He *likes* me. Am I supposed to push him away?"

"*Yes*," Nat hissed, bugging her eyes like Brynn was being totally unreasonable. "That's what we decided this morning, Brynn! You agreed—Priya has dibs."

"What does dibs *mean*?" Brynn demanded. She was getting angry, and she could tell she was raising her voice. But she didn't care. Nobody was around, and besides, this was important. "I thought it meant I was supposed to give Priya a shot. I did, and Ben didn't fall madly in love with her. So am I supposed to stay away from him for the rest of my life?"

Nat narrowed her eyes. "Brynn, come on! We both saw Ben and Priya talking earlier today. They totally hit it off! So are you trying to tell me that he can't possibly like Priya because he's so madly in love with you?"

Brynn sighed. She could hear footsteps around

them, but figured it was just partygoers headed to the (apparently empty) refreshment table, which wasn't too far away. "It's not just that I *think* he doesn't like Priya that way," she said. "It's that he really *doesn't* like Priya that way. He told me. He thinks she's cool as a friend, but that they don't have that much in common."

Brynn heard a branch snap behind her, and turned to see Priya—still soaking wet, and with wide, sad eyes—standing just a few feet behind her. There was no way Priya hadn't heard what she'd just said about her and Ben. Brynn took in a deep breath, feeling her face flush. She felt terrible!

But before she could say more, there were more footsteps nearby, and one of the *actual* counselors for the younger kids stepped up behind Priya.

"*Priya!*" she shouted. "What are you *doing* here, soaking wet? I can't believe you left the tent!"

Priya was still staring at Brynn, like she was letting what she'd just overheard sink in. Slowly, though, her expression turned even sadder, and she turned to face the counselor. "I . . . I just wanted to come to the party for a minute . . ."

The counselor, whose name Brynn thought was Sydney, shook her head. "Well, a minute's all it takes for an emergency to happen. Priya, one of the girls in your bunk woke up feeling very sick. She's got a 102-degree fever, and needs to be brought to the nurse. When she realized you weren't there, she got really scared, and she was crying so hard I heard it from my tent fifty feet away."

Priya gulped. "I didn't mean for anybody . . ."

"Forget it," snapped Sydney. "Just come with me now to talk to Dr. Steve. He's not happy about this."

Priya sighed, but hung her head and followed Sydney. Before she disappeared through the trees, she cast a sad look back at Brynn. Brynn felt her stomach clench. She felt like she'd finally found the boy of her dreams . . . but she'd probably lost a friend in the process.

"Well," Nat said after a moment. "This stinks."

Brynn turned back to face her. "You can say that again."

Nat looked at her, thoughtful. The anger was gone from her eyes and in its place was sympathy—a little for Brynn, maybe, but probably mostly for Priya. "I guess I understand," Nat said, shrugging. "I mean, if Ben's really into you and not Priya, I guess . . ."

Brynn smiled. "I guess we should let him have a say in who he hangs out with?"

Nat grinned. "I *guess*," she said with a sigh. "But you know boys. They're a little dense. Sometimes you have to kind of point them to their destiny."

Brynn laughed. "Yeah, or sometimes they find it all on their own."

In the pit of her stomach, though, she felt a pinch of regret. As much as she liked Ben . . . she really did feel terrible about how it had gone down with Priya. And actually, after their little scene on the raft, who knew if Ben was even still *interested* anymore? He'd run away—swam, actually—from *both* of them pretty fast.

Slowly, she and Nat walked back to the party. For the first time, Brynn noticed that the people hanging around onshore didn't all look *totally* happy. Some of them were shivering. Some were struggling to find their way through the trees in the dark. And a lot of them looked bored. Even though Brynn had thoughtfully set up her iPod to play some tunes, nobody was dancing.

Suddenly Brynn spotted Dr. Steve. He was standing with Sydney and Priya, but when he saw Brynn, he gestured for them to go ahead and started walking over to Brynn.

Brynn swallowed. She had a feeling she knew how this conversation was going to go.

"Well, Brynn," Dr. Steve greeted her. He wasn't smiling, but he wasn't glaring at her, either. She figured that was a good sign.

"Hey, Dr. Steve," she replied, trying to sound cheerful.

"How would you say this party went?" he asked, looking around at a bunch of cold, unhappy campers.

Brynn tried to think of what to say. She'd had a great time—mostly? "I guess I would say it was mostly a success?" she replied.

Dr. Steve nodded. "Well, that's interesting, Brynn. What about the refreshments?" he went on. "Some kids are complaining there was nowhere near enough food for everybody."

Brynn sighed. "Well . . ." The truth was she hadn't been hungry when she'd been planning the party. And she'd been in a rush, so she'd just grabbed whatever she could carry from the mess hall. Still, she had the feeling those weren't the right answers.

"People also seem to think you haven't been

around much," Dr. Steve went on. "All day, really—but especially at the party. So if people had a complaint, they had no way of finding you to let you know."

Brynn didn't say anything this time. She just looked at the ground. "Maybe I'm not cut out to run a camp," she admitted. "I was a little . . . preoccupied."

To her surprise, Dr. Steve didn't take the opportunity to lay into her about how badly she'd done. Instead, he put his hand on her shoulder. "I didn't expect you girls to do a perfect job today," he said simply. "I wanted the day to be a learning experience for you—to see what a big job running this camp really is." He paused. "I think this day has been a learning experience, yes?"

Brynn looked up at him and smiled ruefully. "Definitely."

"Okay then." He backed away. "I've got to get to the nurse's office. We'll talk more tomorrow."

Brynn watched him disappear into the dark woods. She sighed. This day had *definitely* been a learning experience—but had it all been worth it?

Before she could answer that question, someone stepped in front of her. "Hey."

She looked up to see the guy who had inspired her bad behavior that day: Ben. He had dried off a bit, and was wearing a blue T-shirt that said FLYING FLOSSERS, but his hair was still wet. Brynn took a deep breath.

"Hey," she replied.

"So here's the thing," Ben said. "That was a little weird back there."

"I know," Brynn said, her heart sinking, "and I am *so, so* sorry. I never meant for you to feel weird. Priya and I should have talked . . ."

Ben held up his hand for her to stop. "Anyway," he went on, "that doesn't change the fact that I think you are *awesome*. I think you're funny, cute, and we like all the same things. Therefore . . ." he smiled. "I think you should hang out with me," he said quietly. "You know, in a more-than-just-friends sort of way."

Brynn looked into his brown eyes, letting a slow smile spread across her face. "We really *do* have a lot in common," she said. "Because that's exactly what I was thinking."

Ben grinned, putting his arm around her shoulder. Brynn leaned into him, and together they strolled back to the beach, where the moon was hanging *just so* over the glassy lake.

Brynn let out a contented sigh.

At least *something* had gone right on Opposite Day.

chapter THIRTEEN

Jenna sat watching the moon from the bench of a picnic table outside the mess hall. It was totally silent, and a beautiful night. She should have felt at peace, but she didn't. She was just minutes away from attempting to pull off the Prank to End All Pranks, for one thing. And for another . . .

She sighed.

She really had no idea how to feel right now.

In the silence, Jenna suddenly heard someone approaching out of the woods. She didn't look up. She didn't really care who it was. Probably one of her friends coming out from the party, wanting to know why she wasn't there. Didn't she want to have fun with everyone else?

They couldn't understand that she *couldn't* have fun there. Not with David hanging around Sarah the whole time, telling stories in that goofy voice, looking at her all googly-eyed. It wasn't that Jenna wanted David back for herself. She didn't . . . or at least, she was pretty sure she didn't. But seeing him with Sarah? It would just be too weird.

Years and years ago, when Jenna first crushed on David, he'd asked Sarah out first. They'd had a little *thing* that lasted the rest of the summer. They were kind of cute and funny together, but when Jenna and David were reunited and Sarah wasn't around, sparks had flown. And then Sarah hadn't come back to camp the next summer . . . and Jenna had been with David for a long time after.

But maybe David hadn't forgotten about Sarah, and that first summer. Maybe the whole time he and Jenna were together . . .

She bit her lip, hard, stopping her train of thought. She wasn't going to think about this right now. It would just make her cry, and she had a prank to pull off, thank you very much.

But then she heard footsteps drawing closer.

"Hey," said a soft voice. David's voice.

She sighed. "Hey," she replied, turning around a little reluctantly. "How's the party?"

He shrugged. "It's kind of stupid, really," he said, sitting down next to her on the bench. He was still soaking wet, and he sat close enough to get Jenna's pajama bottoms wet, too, actually, but she didn't say anything. "There's, like, no refreshments. I swam for awhile, but then I got bored, and there was nothing else to do." He sighed.

Jenna looked at him, like he was leaving something very important out. "But," she said, forcing the words out, "you must be having fun with Sarah, right?"

David turned to look at Jenna. She usually felt like she understood him pretty well, but right now, she had no idea what he was thinking. His face was totally blank. It was like she'd forgotten to pay her electric bill and the connection went dead. She took a deep breath, almost wishing he wouldn't speak.

"I mean . . ." she stammered, looking away, out at the woods. "You don't have to tell me that stuff. I just . . ."

"I didn't ask Sarah," David said quietly, looking at Jenna with that same unreadable expression. "This afternoon, you kind of took off without telling me how you felt about the whole thing. So I thought maybe you don't *know* how you feel. And then I thought, I can't really be hanging out with one of Jenna's friends without knowing how she feels about it. So I decided to wait. You know, until you decide."

Jenna felt a wave of relief wash over her body. She was pretty sure she didn't want to be David's girlfriend anymore, but at that moment, she could have kissed him. "Thanks," she said quietly, and David just nodded, and for awhile they looked out at the woods together.

It was silent for a minute or two, but it was a comfortable silence. Two people quietly thinking their own thoughts on a warm, summer night. Finally Jenna said, "I don't think I want to get back together. So maybe it's not fair to keep you from being with someone else. It's just . . . it's hard to think of you as someone else's boyfriend. Even Sarah . . . even though you were her boyfriend before." She gulped.

David nodded slowly. "I get it," he agreed. "If it were the other way around, and you wanted to date

Ben or something, I'd probably be pretty weirded out by that."

Jenna chuckled. "Actually, I think I'm the only person in my bunk who *doesn't* want to date Ben," she said.

David laughed. "That guy," he muttered. "If I knew, all this time, the key to having girls fall all over me was a haircut . . ."

Jenna laughed harder. As long as she knew him, David had been crowned by a floppy, messy batch of dark hair. "I wouldn't cut it," she choked out between laughs. "It's your signature."

David smiled at her. "I guess you're right."

After a few minutes, Jenna got control of herself, and she turned to David with a grateful smile. "Thanks," she said. "For caring about how I feel."

David shrugged. "Of course," he said. "Just because we're not going out anymore doesn't mean I don't care what you think. You're, like, my favorite person, Jenna."

Jenna nodded. "Thanks." She leaned in and gave him a hug. "And you're probably mine."

Just then, Jenna heard a shout from the lake. *Brynn!*

"I repeat, the party is over!" Brynn shouted. "Please head back to your tents!"

Jenna looked at David, thrilled and terrified at the same time. "You know what that means . . ." she said.

David sprung up from the bench. "The Prank to End All Pranks!" he whispered fiercely.

Immediately, they sprung into action. Jenna didn't

even have to tell David what to do, they'd rehearsed it so many times. They both ran over to the mess hall and carefully dragged out the garbage bags full of water balloons they'd arranged near the door. After a few minutes, Sarah and Sloan came running out to help, and slowly, the other members of Jenna's bunk filtered out of the woods and helped move the balloons. By the time the first campers came casually strolling down the path that led through the woods to the lake, all ten bunkmates, plus David, Ben, and the other boys from their bunk, were all lined up, armed and ready.

"*Cowabunga!!!*" screamed Jenna, winging two water balloons at a couple of unsuspecting seventh-grade boys. Both balloons exploded with a satisfying *Sploosh!*, and the boys gasped, totally caught off guard . . . and then *totally* wanting revenge.

"What the heck?" one cried. "I'm totally getting you back for that!"

"Here," called David, handing the boy some balloons from a nearby bag. "She hates getting hit in the face! Have at it!"

Jenna glared at him, but she had to run to duck from the balloons before she could get him back. For the next few minutes, campers continued to stream down the path, and it was messy, wet, divine chaos. Jenna did manage to nail David with a few balloons—but he got her back, too.

After a few minutes, Dr. Steve came running out of his office, trailed by one of the younger kids' counselors, and—was that *Priya?* Priya shrieked and immediately grabbed a balloon, and Dr. Steve just watched for a few minutes, his jaw hanging open. He shook his head like he couldn't believe what he was seeing.

"Are you going to stop this?" the counselor asked, watching the chaos like she wasn't quite sure what to do.

Dr. Steve seemed to consider this for a moment, then shook his head. "I can't," he replied. "For better or worse . . . Jenna's bunk is still in charge."

Just then, one of the braver seventh-graders threw a balloon at Dr. Steve, soaking his pajamas from the chest down. Dr. Steve shook his head. "Oh, no, you don't," he warned. "I'm still a camper until midnight, and I don't think any of my campers would let that go." Jenna tossed him a balloon, and he caught her eye for a second, mouthing, "Big! Trouble! Tomorrow!" But Jenna didn't care. This prank was everything she'd hoped it would be, and as Dr. Steve went after the seventh-grader with a fat, red balloon, she was pretty sure she was experiencing the best moment of her life.

It was at least half an hour before all the balloons were gone and the campers, soaking wet and exhausted, were herded back to their tents.

For a few moments, Jenna and her bunkmates were alone on the drenched, muddy yard, watching "their" campers being led away. Jasmine and Jamie, posing as "campers," had long since wandered back to the tent, so for just a few last minutes, Jenna and her friends were able to savor being in charge.

"That," said Jenna as her friends gathered round, "was the best night of my life. Thank you so much, guys."

Sarah smiled. "No problem, Jenna. It was pretty awesome."

Jenna looked at Sarah and gave her a little smile of thanks. It was going to be hard to act normal around her for awhile, knowing how David felt—but she knew deep down, she liked Sarah too much to let anything get in the way of their friendship. She hoped, whatever happened, they could all stay friends.

As they slowly started walking back to the tent, Brynn suddenly wandered over to Priya.

"Priya," she said. "I just want to . . . I'm so sorry . . . I never . . ."

Priya turned to Brynn and sighed an exhausted sigh. "Forget it, Brynn," she said, shaking her head with a little smile. "I really liked Ben, but I *can't* be mad at you if he really likes you better. It hurt for me to hear it that way, but maybe I needed to. I totally get it now."

Brynn sighed, nodding. "Still," she said. "I should have been straight with you from the beginning. Not sneaking around trying to plan ways to be with Ben. I guess I got a little high on my own power."

Chelsea laughed. "You're not the only one, Brynn," she said. "Look at my lunch debacle. I thought if I liked something, everybody else would just deal with it. But look how wrong I was. Nat says there were kids in her bunks who didn't speak to each other the whole rest of the day because of where they sat at lunch."

"And I decided all the kids should try oil painting in Arts and Crafts—because that's what real artists use," Avery added, shaking her head. "Let's just say, it got kind of messy."

"How messy?" asked Jenna.

"*So* messy that I think parents will be complaining about the whole outfits their kids destroyed," Avery admitted.

Sloan gasped. "Didn't you make them use smocks?" she asked.

"Smocks?" asked Avery. "Why didn't I think of that?"

Everyone chuckled.

"Well," said Priya, "I kind of got in over my head, too. I don't think I'm cut out to work with little kids."

Brynn nodded. "And I don't think I'm cut out to run a camp."

Jenna shrugged. "I am *totally* cut out to plan the most rockin' pranks this camp has ever seen," she said. "Oh. But not to do . . . well, whatever I was *supposed* to be doing today."

Nat snorted. "Well, kids, I hope we all enjoyed Opposite Day," she said. "Because in just an hour or two, we go back to a plain, old, normal, Camp Walla Walla Day."

Priya sighed. "I can't *wait*," she admitted. "And I think I might sleep in my regular clothes tonight. Seriously, enough pajamas!"

chapter FOURTEEN

To: chacelvr@fastmail.net
From: priyadayada@internet.com
Re: Ya win some . . .

Hey Jules,

Okaaaaay, sooooo . . .

It turns out love is not all it's cracked up to be.

Some things happened last night. I'm not going to go into detail. Let's just say decisions were made, the were all bad, and I kind of got my head handed to me in lecture form by a couple of counselors.

Oh, and Ben doesn't like me that way. He likes my friend Brynn. Isn't that just the icing on the cake?

Still, I'm trying to make the best of things. You know me: Positive Priya. We had this huge water-balloo fight last night, and I got to talk to Jordan a little (after nailing him in the face with a balloon, ha!!), and he reminded me that I'm awesome and don't need to be wasting my time on guys that don't see that.

Even if they are gorgeous and awesome.

(That last part is from me, not from Jordan.)

Seriously, though . . . I'm setting my sights higher next time. If this little experience has shown me anything, it's that I'm ready for romance. Bring it on! But this time, I'm after a sweet, optimistic, fun guy who cares about others (sometimes maybe too much), and is suddenly way interested in photography.

Sound familiar??

Love ya, Jules—and hope you're having a better week than me!

Priya!!

It wasn't exactly a surprise when Dr. Steve asked for all the members of Priya's bunk to come meet him in his office after breakfast the next day.

Priya had gotten a nice, long lecture last night . . . but the Prank to End All Pranks (a name that seemed to be catching on among all the campers, to Jenna's delight) had interrupted it before she could be given any sort of punishment. Now, she had a feeling she was in even bigger trouble than before. And while Dr. Steve had joined in the fun last night as a "camper," Priya had a feeling the "real" Dr. Steve wouldn't be quite so mellow.

"What do you think he's going to do to us?" Chelsea asked, biting nervously on her thumbnail as they all walked to Dr. Steve's office.

"I'm not sure," said Sarah, looking thoughtful. "Make us clean up the mess hall after every meal for a week? No dessert for a month?"

Nat sighed. "I've seen him give those punishments before, but this almost seems bigger than that. I just hope he doesn't call our parents. My dad is right in the middle of a promotional tour."

Avery groaned. "If they call our parents, mine will ground me for a month when we get home."

Jenna shook her head. "Ladies, ladies," she said with a sigh. "I don't think you get it. Dr. Steve could boil us in oil, but we still would have pulled off the most amazing prank in camp history last night!"

Brynn laughed. "Jenna. When are you going to come down from your prank high?"

Jenna smiled. "Never," she replied. "You don't understand, Brynn. This is like the holy grail of the prank world." She paused, her face turning serious. "Although . . . guys?"

Nat glanced back at her, a little surprised. "What?"

Jenna bit her lip, then went on, "I'm . . . you know . . . I'm sorry if I got a little crazy yesterday. I know I can be a little . . ."

"Bossy?" Avery interjected.

Jenna nodded. "Yeah. The b-word. I'm sorry. I don't mean to upset you guys . . . I was just so, *so* excited about this prank." She paused, looking up brightly. "I promise to be better about the next prank."

Nat broke out laughing. "Jenna!" she cried. "You say that *every* time!"

Jenna smiled. "But this time I mean it!"

Everyone chuckled, but they were reaching the

end of their walk. Sloan sighed. "Well, guys. This is it."
They were standing in front of Dr. Steve's office. "Let's
face our destiny together."

Inside, Dr. Steve was waiting for them. They all
trooped into his office, where he sat behind his desk,
looking equal parts upset and amused.

"Girls," he said. "We had a very exciting day
yesterday."

"We certainly did," agreed Jenna.

"Maybe *too* exciting at times," added Brynn.

Dr. Steve nodded. "How did you find the process
of running the camp?"

Brynn laughed. *"Difficult?"* she asked. "But that's an
understatement. Dr. Steve, I learned I never want your
job."

He laughed. *"Touché,"* he replied, smiling at Brynn.
"How about the rest of you?"

"It was harder than I thought it would be,"
admitted Chelsea. "Turns out, you really have to think
about what a bunch of kids might want to eat. They're
picky."

"Right," agreed Avery. "And, um, they're not
exactly so neat with the oil paint. Or so understanding
about their clothes getting messed up."

Priya nodded. "And little kids are just . . . hard."

Everyone laughed at that. Dr. Steve nodded
sympathetically. "You can say that again, Priya," he
agreed. "I think you learned that the hard way."

Priya blushed, suddenly reminded of her poor
behavior the night before. She hoped she wasn't going
to get the whole bunk in trouble.

"Well," Dr. Steve went on, "there were lots of little bumps in the road, but for most of you, it was nothing you could have been expected to foresee. Part of what I wanted your bunk to learn on Opposite Day was that a lot of time and care goes into running this camp."

Brynn nodded. "For real," she agreed.

"But *some* of you," Dr. Steve went on, "made unusually poor decisions. Priya, you chose to leave the younger kids you were supposed to be watching."

Priya looked down at the floor.

"Brynn," Dr. Steve went on, "you were responsible for some hasty planning and some unhappy campers."

Brynn nodded, looking uncomfortable. "I know, sir."

"And you," Dr. Steve added, looking right at Jenna. "You were responsible for the worst abuse of authority of all. Jenna, did you even *interact* with your campers all day? Or was the whole day dedicated to preparing for your little prank?"

Jenna looked at her friends, then back at Dr. Steve. "With all due respect, sir, that was no *little* prank."

Dr. Steve snorted. "Oh, just answer the question."

Jenna grinned. "I prepared all day," she replied. "But I didn't think that was so bad because the older campers can take care of themselves. Thank goodness Priya switched with me, or I would have had to throw in the towel. There's no way I could have pulled this off if I had been watching the little kids."

Dr. Steve looked at Priya. "That's right," he said. "You *did* switch with Jenna. Which doesn't totally excuse your behavior . . . but maybe it casts some light on your lack of little kid skills, you might say."

Priya blushed and looked away.

"Dr. Steve," Brynn spoke up now. "I just want to say I'm really sorry for the way I acted. It was selfish, and I get now that it wasn't fair to the rest of the camp. It won't happen again. You know, if we ever do another Opposite Day."

"Me too," agreed Priya. "I mean, it's probably not enough, but I want you to know I *am* sorry. I never wanted those kids to get hurt or feel scared."

Dr. Steve nodded, turning to face Jenna. "And?" he asked.

Jenna looked pained. She seemed to be trying to get the words out, but failing. "Oh, Dr. Steve," she said after a few seconds. "I can't lie. I still think it was *totally* worth it! I know you're mad, but, dude—I pulled off the best prank in Camp Walla Walla history! The Prank to End All Pranks!"

Jenna's bunkmates looked a little sheepishly at Dr. Steve. There was no arguing with Jenna's enthusiasm—but they knew a punishment was coming.

A smile passed over Dr. Steve's face, but he quickly grew serious again. "In that case," he said, "you won't mind cleaning up all the broken balloons on the lawn, Jenna. That's how you'll spend all day today. Then your debt will be paid, and we can forget Opposite Day ever happened."

Priya looked around at her bunkmates. They all looked dismayed. Poor Jenna, getting punished for a prank they'd all helped out on! After a moment, Priya cleared her throat and stepped forward. "With all due respect, Dr. Steve," she said, "it was really *all* of us who helped pull off the prank. And our bunk hangs together. If Jenna's punished, we all should be punished."

Chelsea stepped forward, nodding. "I agree," she said.

"Yeah," agreed Avery, nodding, too. "If you're going to punish Jenna . . . punish all of us. We want to stand together."

Dr. Steve looked from Priya to the rest of the girls, who were all nodding in agreement. "Very well then," he agreed, looking pleased. "You can all start cleaning the lawn right . . . *now!*"

The girls made their way back onto the balloon-strewn lawn with huge garbage bags to pick up the broken balloon pieces. It didn't take long for all of the girls to realize it was not nearly as much fun as throwing the balloons had been—throwing broken balloon pieces at each other just didn't work very well. And they had to keep bending down in the hot sun, and the lawn was huge and completely covered.

Still, though, they were together.

"Totally worth it," muttered Jenna about forty-five minutes into their shift. She was met by a hail of broken balloon pieces and dirty grass as her bunkmates all moved on her, flinging whatever they had in their hands. Jenna burst out laughing, and the other girls were quick to follow.

Priya couldn't help smiling, watching them all. Maybe romance had eluded her this time around—but thank goodness she still had her friends.

Here's a sneak preview of

camp
CONFIDENTIAL

IN IT TO WIN IT

available soon!

chapter ONE

As soon as Sloan typed a *w* in the Google search box, weatherwatch.com came up in her browser history. Right at the top. She'd been compulsively checking the site for a day and a half, looking for a prediction that would make her parents change their minds and give her the okay to fly off to the Walla Walla reunion over Presidents' Day weekend.

Please, please, please, she thought as she clicked it, then typed in the zip code for the Connecticut lodge where the reunion was going to be held. Holding her breath, she scanned the ten-day forecast. There was a sixty-five percent chance of a snowstorm over the long weekend—same as when she'd checked the site yesterday.

Sloan let out the breath. Sixty-five percent. Those odds weren't so bad, and she couldn't wait to see if they would get better. It was time to go make her plea to her parents.

But first—She jumped over to the camp blog. She'd posted a message asking for advice on the parent sitch, and she wanted to see if any of her friends had come up with anything. She smiled when she saw Avery had posted an answer. Avery was good at getting what she wanted. Sloan eagerly read the message.

Posted by: Avery
Subject: Doom

Sloan, here's my advice: Whine and beg. Maybe pout a little. (But not so much that you make your parents so mad, they'll never say yes.) If you can do it right, cry some. Play your parents against each other. Basically, just manipulate, manipulate, manipulate.

Hmmm. Sloan wasn't a drama kind of girl. She was pretty sure that she couldn't squeeze out even one really good fake tear.

Jenna had posted a reply, too. She wasn't the actress type, either. Maybe her advice would be easier to follow. Sloan clicked on her message and read it.

Posted by: Jenna
Subject: Doom

My dad is a stats guy. The stats look okay, he's okay. Use them on your parents, Sloan.

And remember, if you don't get your behind to the lodge, I will hunt you down. And it won't be fun! And it won't be pretty!

I threaten cuz I love.

Statistics Sloan could handle. She checked a few more websites and memorized a few facts that she thought could help her make her case, then she headed to the kitchen. Her mom was pulling a tofu lasagna out of the oven. Her dad was tossing one of his special salads, this one with cranberries and pecans. Sloan hesitated in the doorway, watching them. *I think it's safe for me to fly to Connecticut.* That's what she meant to say. But the words that came out of her mouth were, "I think I'll make us fuzzy orange smoothies to go with dinner."

This made her parents happy because they loved Sloan's smoothies. She walked over to the fridge and started pulling out Greek yogurt and the other ingredients she'd need. Why was she so nervous? Her parents were hardly beasts.

Sloan knew the answer. Her parents weren't beastly, but they still might not change their minds. They might give Sloan the no again. And Sloan wasn't ready to hear it if they did. She couldn't wait all the way until summer to see her camp friends again. That was months and months away—forever in friend time.

Okay, during dinner, while they're enjoying the smoothies, I'll ask, Sloan promised herself. As she began to put orange sections into the blender, the back door flew open. Willow, Sloan's aunt, rushed in.

"I got the last loaf of rosemary bread. Score!" She waved her mesh shopping bag over her head in triumph.

"I didn't know you were coming for dinner," Sloan

said, grabbing some cinnamon from the cabinet above the blender.

"I invited myself right this second," Willow answered. "But I brought bread. That means I'm welcome."

"You're always welcome. Knowing you, you'd never eat if you didn't want to see us once in a while," Sloan's mom told her. Willow was her younger sister, and sometimes her mom acted like Willow was younger than Sloan.

"You're right. I couldn't live without you. I'd wither away." Willow gave Sloan's mom a hug, shooting a wink at Sloan.

"Very funny. I give out love and concern and I get mocked for it," Sloan's mom said, trying to sound mad, but smiling. "Okay, everyone, let's get the food on the table."

Sloan poured the smoothie mix into four glasses and carried them to the big table that dominated one side of the huge main room. She loved the big, old table, especially the way it matched the massive exposed beams of the ceiling. But as much as she loved the room, and her parents, and her aunt, and tofu lasagna, and fuzzy orange smoothies, she felt nervous. *Not beasts*, she reminded herself, taking her usual seat.

A conversation started up about the new sculpture being installed in Sedona's arts and crafts village. Sloan *uh-huh*ed and *mm-hmm*ed her way through it, not able to concentrate. She was shocked when she realized she was halfway through her lasagna and had finished her salad. She didn't remember tasting a bite.

Do it! she ordered herself. *Just do it, or dinner will be over and any smoothie magic you had going will be gone.* "I have something I wanted to talk to you about," she blurted.

"You just interrupted your aunt," her dad pointed out.

"Sorry, Willow," Sloan said. "What were you saying?"

"Doesn't matter. From the look on your face, you have something important going on," Willow answered.

"I . . . You . . . Weatherwatch . . ." She'd lost contact with the part of her brain that could form sentences. She took a breath, then tried again. "I wanted to let you know that the weather forecast is predicting a sixty-five percent chance of snow in Connecticut over the long weekend. That's not bad, right? Sixty-five percent?"

Willow's eyes began to gleam. "In 2002, there was a freak snowstorm in North Carolina. There was only an eight percent chance it would hit, but it did. Knocked out electricity all over the place. I didn't know you'd gotten into meteorology," she added.

"She's gotten into wanting to go to her camp reunion," Sloan's dad said, smiling sympathetically at Sloan.

"Of course. I don't know why I didn't make that connection right away when you said *Connecticut*," Willow answered.

Her aunt was an extreme weather junkie. Sloan hadn't factored that in when she was prepping for this conversation, because she hadn't expected Willow to be there. Maybe she could turn it to her advantage.

"There probably won't be a snowstorm, but if there is, it could be awesome to experience it, right, Willow? You go all over the place chasing storms so you can see the"—Sloan searched her mind for the phrase her aunt always used—"wildness and majesty of nature."

Sloan's mother groaned. "Please don't use your aunt as an example of sensible behavior," she said.

"Only forty people died last year from a lightning strike!" Sloan exclaimed, trying a new tactic. Her parents and Willow stared at her. Oh, wait. Wrong statistic. *Get it together,* she ordered herself. "I mean, only four hundred forty-nine people died of hypothermia."

"We aren't worried you're going to freeze to death, Sloan," her dad said.

"Well, we are a little," her mother corrected.

"But we're more worried about things like your connecting plane being delayed by the weather," Sloan's dad continued. "We don't want you sitting all by yourself in an airport in a city where you know no one."

"Or getting snowed in at that lodge, which is in the middle of nowhere," her mother added.

So much for stats, Sloan thought. She decided to try a little of Avery's advice. "Please let me go. Just please." *I'm not all that good at begging,* she realized.

To her surprise, her father turned to her mother. "I checked a couple weather sites, too," he told her.

"Like Sloan said, there's only little more than a fifty-fifty chance there will be a snowstorm. And if there is, it's not a given that any of the airports will have to delay flights more than a few hours."

"We've already decided this. She's not going," Sloan's mom protested.

"Maybe we should rethink it," he said.

Yes, yes, yes! Sloan thought. "What do you think, Willow?" she asked. She didn't want to play her parents against each other. But getting her aunt to agree with her dad couldn't hurt.

Willow didn't answer. She was fiddling with her Blackberry. "What do you think, Willy?" Sloan asked again.

Willow frowned, eyes still on her Blackberry screen. "Connecticut had unusually hot weather summer before last," she said.

"See! Unusually warm weather! That means no snow!" Sloan cried.

"Actually, it means the opposite. Many times where there's an unusually hot summer someplace there is an unusually bad winter there sixteen months later," Willow said. She shook her head. "I'm not happy with what I'm seeing on bird migration patterns. Hibernation data, either. And the wind patterns— cold wind is going to be shooting into Connecticut over the weekend. I don't think that there's a sixty-five percent chance of a snowstorm. I think there's more like a ninety-eight percent chance." She looked over at Sloan. "Sorry, sweetie. But the birds and bears know the score."

"Willow agrees with me," Sloan's mom said."It's settled."

"No. Wait!" Tears actually did begin to sting Sloan's eyes as she thought about missing the chance to be with her friends. There had to be a way to turn this around.